Follies, Fables and Fantasy

Follies, Fables and Fantasy

Animal Adventures and Fairy Tales from the South West

ENDYMION BEER

children's hospice
SOUTH WEST
Registered Charity No. 1003314

ryelands

First published in Great Britain in 2009

British Library Cataloguing-in-Publication Data
A CIP record for this title is available from the British Library

ISBN 978 1 906551 21 6

RYELANDS
Halsgrove House,
Ryelands Industrial Estate,
Bagley Road, Wellington, Somerset TA21 9PZ
Tel: 01823 653777   Fax: 01823 216796
email: sales@halsgrove.com

Part of the Halsgrove group of companies
Information on all Halsgrove titles is available at: www.halsgrove.com

Printed and bound by The Shortrun Press, Exeter

A Note From The Author

I would like to thank Trevor Beer MBE for illustrating the first two stories of this book. Trevor originally produced these illustrations for a dummy book I had produced before I was properly illustrating but now the project is considerably larger! The remaining stories were all illustrated by me. I'd also like to thank my good friend Vincent for the idea of the Dachshund running away to live with the badgers in 'The Magnificent Adventures of Toby'.

The Magnificent Adventures are for slightly older readers, although the stories are written for the whole family to enjoy. It is hoped that perhaps younger members of the family and their friends might be read to. Specific human characters have deliberately not been illustrated since it is sometimes preferred that the reader can portray his/herself as the hero/heroine of the story.

I'd especially like to thank Halsgrove for making this project possible. 100% of the profits from the sale of this book will go towards the charity Children's Hospice South West. For this reason I have located each story locally so that children may relate to specific places.

Finally thank you to the North Devon School of Art for bringing me up to speed with multi-media and illustration skills.

Sponsorship for *Follies, Fables and Fantasy* – A Children's Hospice South West Project

Trevor Beer MBE, Countryside Matters, Barnstaple
Paul Rendell, Dartmoor News Magazine, Okehampton
Mick Gover, Gover's, Barnstaple
Mr R S Beer Bookseller, Barnstaple
Stuart Christophers, Parnell Lang Enterprises Ltd
Mrs M A Maguire, Exmouth
J&A Cameras, Barnstaple, Bideford, Tiverton
Mr Trevor Dunn, Barnstaple
Mole Valley Farmers Forage Services
Muddiford Inn, Muddiford, Nr Barnstaple
Mrs R D Beer, Barnstaple
Tony Draper Plant Hire Ltd, Combe Martin
Endymion Beer, Naturama, Barnstaple

Dedication:
To Absent Friends.

Foreword

This charming collection of short stories brings to life the hidden world which lurks just beyond the eyes of most of us – in the depths of our rich English countryside.

Weaving together her vivid imagination with all she has learned exploring the countryside and wildlife with Trevor Beer MBE, the celebrated and award-winning Devon naturalist, the writer is a natural story teller with a great empathy for the little "people".

Her principle characters, like Bracken the border collie, Holly the German shepherd, Foggy the grey and white cat, the police mouse PC Timothy Truncheon, Willow the sheep dog, Spinney the squirrel, and even some human children, come from a world with which we are all familiar.

But they transport us into fantasy worlds where as well as rubbing shoulders with Devon's wildlife – badgers, otters, stoats and weasels – they also tangle with fairies, Robber Flies, mermaids, Jack Frost, nymphs who give counselling, M.I.7's flies looking for traitors, Neptune the sea god, arsonists, Mouseketeers, talking beetles and a Wicked Witch.

Readers familiar with North Devon will recognise the settings for these stories: Braunton Burrows, Woody Bay, Hidden Valley, Barnstaple's castle mound, Anchor Wood, the Tarka Trail, the Black Venus on Exmoor and the Taw estuary.

Those who don't know the area will surely feel a pull to visit North Devon – recognised by the Campaign for the Protection of Rural England as one of the six last tranquil places in the country, and by the United Nations as so special they have designated it a World Biosphere Reserve.

Whether as a Christmas stocking-filler, a holiday read or a children's bedtime story, these absorbing tales will give pleasure to people of all ages – and a fascinating insight to the world around us.

NICK HARVEY
Member of Parliament for North Devon

Contents

The Adventures of Bracken

Bracken on the Burrows

The sand dunes glowed warmly in the midsummer sunshine. Foggy yawned and promptly washed her pink nose and long whiskers. She was a pretty little white and grey cat and quite shy.

"Atishoo!" She sneezed.

Bracken the Border collie dog pricked up his ears, opened one eye and then the other. Yes his little friend was alright, just sneezing so he closed his eyes once again.

'Bump!' Now his eyes were suddenly open and he looked up with a start as Foggy affectionately head butted him. Bracken wagged his tail happily.

"What shall we do today?" He asked her yawning.

"I want to see the sea", she purred marching off to the 'Board Walk' and so Bracken followed loyally.

"This is like the yellow brick road." She said skipping and jumping about. Bracken chuckled and told her the Board Walk was made to stop people walking on the flowers.

Suddenly shimmering in the sun, Foggy thought she'd found treasure! When they looked closer they discovered it was a mermaid's purse.

"Oh do let me keep it Bracken." Foggy pleaded.

"Hmmmmm…." He said thinking.

The purse was covered in silvery green fish scale sequins all sewn on with spider's silk. After finding the name 'Pearly' embroidered in the centre it was quite obvious that Foggy couldn't keep the purse because it belonged to somebody. So it was agreed they must find the owner and give it back.

"But how do we do that if it really does belong to a mermaid?" Foggy asked.

"We must find Neptune and ask his advice replied Bracken wisely. And off they went to find the sea.

"I can see the sea! I can see the sea!" Foggy chanted standing on Bracken's back. She raced off to the beach excitedly but Bracken couldn't answer her because he was carrying the purse in his mouth. Foggy pawed playfully at some shells and then pounced on a large clump of seaweed that started to move sideways underneath her.

"Oh my! Bracken help!" she shouted.

Bracken dropped the purse and picked Foggy up by the scruff of her neck. His tail caught in some of the seaweed and when they looked back all they saw was a rather cross looking crab. The crab pulled its seaweed back over itself mumbling and disappeared from view again. But in all the commotion Bracken had dropped the purse but when he went to fetch it a huge seagull swooped down and snatched it up! As they watched the seagull soar up into the sky it appeared to land on the back of a shaggy black crow, but just as it landed the seagull changed into a little black imp. The imp waved the purse at Bracken cackling as he rode away on his crow.

"Treagle!" growled Bracken.

"Who?" Foggy exclaimed.

"Treagle the imp up to no good again," he replied.

Bracken and Foggy searched the beach for a conch, a special shell they needed to summon Neptune. They searched the beach until the sun began to sink and the sky turned red.

"Atishoo!" said something.

Bracken and Foggy looked at each other, neither of them had sneezed.

"Atishoo! Atishoo! Atishoo!"

It was a rabbit who suddenly lost his balance, tumbled down a huge sand dune onto the beach and bumped into Bracken's legs.

"Whoops!" exclaimed the rabbit.

Bump! Another rabbit bumped into Bracken's legs.

"Are you going to eat us Sir?" asked the second rabbit with very wide eyes. Bracken chuckled and explained that he was not a fox and didn't eat rabbits.

"Phew!" they sighed.

Bracken and Foggy on the beach

The rabbits said their names were Gowan and Gossamer and that they'd been playing in the dunes with clock dandelions when the wind had blown the wrong way causing Gowan to sneeze as the fluffy seeds of dandelion tickled his nose. Gossamer thought it was very funny indeed and began to giggle again. Suddenly their eyes grew very wide and their mouths opened in terror.

"Look!" cried Gowan.

"Oh my!" shrieked Gossamer as both rabbits disappeared back up into the dunes again, their cotton tails bobbing as they fled. Foggy and Bracken looked over their shoulders to see a raging tide coming in very fast.

"Run!" barked Bracken and he and Foggy made it to the safety of the dunes just in time.

"That was a close one….," panted Foggy with her ears pointing backwards. "… but look what I found!" she added excitedly and presenting a conch to Bracken. Bracken was so happy he howled to the now rising moon and blew the conch to sound a magical note.

There was a low rumble of thunder and the sea began to boil as something stirred beneath it. The waves lapped around the foot of the dunes and white horses broke before them. Whoooosh! Neptune emerged from the sea holding his trident.

"You summoned me. Why?" His voice boomed and echoed through the dunes. Foggy hid behind Bracken's tail and clung to his back legs. Bracken told Neptune their story about the purse.

"And where is the purse now?" Neptune asked.

"Treagle stole it sire", whispered Foggy from behind Bracken's legs.

"What?…… Treagle!" Neptune raised his trident and a huge flash of lightning crashed through the night sky.

"One of my Princesses, Princess Pearly of the mermaids is missing. We can now assume she had been abducted". Neptune explained.

"By whom… Treagle?" asked Bracken.

"Well, I suspect Jack Frost is holding her captive. Treagle was probably summoned from the Underworld to aid him. Princess Pearly is to become Queen of the Selkies next moon. The King of the Selkies will arrive tomorrow to take her back to his kingdom in preparation for their wedding. You see, Jack Frost wanted to marry Pearly against her will but of course I forbade it. I am certain Jack Frost has her". Neptune's eyes grew intensely sad.

"Cor! Cor! Cor!" cried a shaggy black crow.

"Catch!" cried Treagle's rasping voice as he threw a green bottle into the sea containing a note.

Neptune raised his trident ready to destroy Treagle but Treagle shrieked from the back of his crow….

"If I do not return, Jack Frost will destroy Pearly!" and with that he picked up the reins, jerked them, and the shaggy black crow flew away just as the ghostly white of a barn owl swooped before Neptune. Neptune's eyes sparkled gold to the barn owl that blinked in response and disappeared winging away across the sea.

Neptune sighed, retrieved the runic script from the bottle and read it to himself. Then, he blew into a sea green horn that he kept tied about his waist and summoned the Mermaid People, Water Nymphs and all the seals in the land. He announced Pearly's abduction telling them that Jack Frost had demanded power over them all including the seas and water worlds.

"In other words, he wants my throne!" roared Neptune and everyone gasped.

"Skreee, skreee, skreee, Seal Point," called Alba the barn owl appearing as if from nowhere.

Neptune smiled explaining he had had Alba follow Treagle to reveal where they were holding Pearly. Then he prepared his people for the arrival of The King of Selkies and told the seals of an amazing plan which they would have to keep secret until the morning. He then sent the mermaid people to his palace to guard it in preparation for their special guest, and ordered the water nymphs to entertain the King.

"We will need his help", said Neptune.

They talked and planned until the moon was at its highest and waited for Treagle to return to take back Neptune's decision. Everyone hid so that Treagle wouldn't suspect anything was afoot.

"My decision is that Jack Frost can take my throne if he can prove himself worthy. He must freeze the world for three days and three nights. If he succeeds he can take my throne. Now send Pearly back", commanded Neptune.

"Never!" cackled Treagle. "Jack Frost has changed his mind. He wants your throne *and* Pearly!" And Treagle vanished.

Foggy was now asleep between Bracken's front paws. Something was prodding her. She woke up to find a Gnome standing before her.

"My people want to help", announced the Gnome.

Neptune overheard and asked the Gnome how he thought he could help.

"Well Sire, my people live in the heart of the dunes and it is a long way for us to travel on foot to Seal Point, but if we rode Bracken and Foggy we could get there in half the time". said the Gnome who proceeded to tell Neptune of his plan.

Just then, a mermaid announced that the Selkie King had arrived early. He had been informed of the situation and was anxious not to waste any time. Now Selkie People take the form of seals when they are in the water so they changed places with all the seals who lived locally. The grey seals were very excited because they were being treated to hide in Neptune's Palace.

Bracken and Foggy set off with 13 Gnomes riding on their backs. Each held a crystal lantern and carried the magical fern seed that made them invisible. Jack Frost would not be expecting attack by land, he would expect it to come from the sea but it was wise to take precautions for he was a dangerous character. And so began the journey to Seal Point. It wasn't far but it was dangerous.

Meanwhile at Seal Point an army of conger eels were patrolling the sea and two electric eels guarded the underwater cave entrance. Muffled voices drifted up through the water.

"I have won Princess Pearly! Neptune has given in to my supreme powers." announced Jack Frost in his coldly sharp voice.

"You will never break my spirit Jack Frost for I will never believe a word you say", replied Pearly firmly.

A conger eel began to laugh hysterically.

"Be gone… be gone I say… and keep watch!" Cried Jack Frost who was so angry his face went red with temper.

"Yes master," wailed the fearful eel.

The conger eel left the blue crystal cave of stalagmites and stalactites made of ice and frost. The ice portcullis was raised to let him out and an electric eel gave him a nasty shock just for the fun of it.

"Fool, don't you know I'm bigger than you", said the angry conger eel swimming away swishing his tail fiercely.

Outside Treagle was surveying the land and sea from the back of his shaggy black crow. His beady eyes were sharp, missing nothing as he scanned the terrain. Bracken and Foggy had almost reached Seal Point so the Gnomes quickly jumped off and silently moved to form a tight circle above the underwater cave. Just then Jack Frost cast his spell to freeze the land.

The leaves became frosted and the land turned white. The air was suddenly sharp to breathe.

"Hurry…. Set the lanterns down!" ordered the Gnome leader.

Bracken and Foggy watched as the crystals became brighter and hotter when they were placed together. There was a low hum and the frost began to melt as quickly as it appeared. Suddenly the magical fern seed wore off and the little party became visible to Treagle who immediately charged at them on his crow. When the crow was just above Bracken's head, he barked. The crow jumped and Treagle fell tumbling through the air only to be caught by the gnomes in a large sticky spider's web. The crow flew away shrieking fearfully.

Down by the sea the seals were in position. Undetected by Jack Frost's guards who thought they were the harmless local seals they were able to swim right up to the cave entrance. The portcullis had just begun to weaken from the heat of the magical lanterns and without warning the Selkie People charged forward smashing it. There was nothing the guards could do for they were outnumbered and were all captured. Instantly, Jack Frost's icy spell was broken and the sea and land returned to normal much to the relief of all the wild creatures. Then the Selkie People changed from seals into their true form. Neptune arrived and gave Jack Frost the worst punishment he could ever have dreamed of….. to spend a year with the sun goddess to learn humility before he could return to Earth. His spells of ice would be powerless with her.

The Selkie King embraced Pearly.
"You will never leave my side again, not even for a minute!" he said.
"My love!" she cried.
And Neptune's People cheered as tears of joy rolled down Pearly's face.
"Let the celebrations begin!" announced Neptune as strange watery music seemed to swirl all about them.

Later, Princess Pearly presented Foggy with her purse to keep as a token of her gratitude. What a great honour! Princess Pearly also shared the secrets of her people with Bracken and Foggy as a token of her trust and told them they could come and go whenever they pleased. However, weary they had felt, they now had a new lease of life and joined in with the celebrations at Neptune's Palace. And so the world was now at peace and safe from the perils of Jack Frost once more.

THE END

Bracken & The Boggart

"Pink! Pink! Pink!" Cried the blackbirds as Foggy sat beneath the hawthorn tree. She was deaf to their alarm call and was only interested in the large beetle waddling across the path in front of her. On hearing the blackbirds alarm calls Bracken came charging down the path towards Foggy.

"I hope you're not upsetting *my* blackbirds", he said sternly.

She didn't answer him and he soon realised she was transfixed by the large beetle ambling along with its tatty wings. Foggy's ears were pointing forward, listening to the slightest sound, and her tail twitched in anticipation. She was quite oblivious to any other sound. Bracken wanted to know what was so fascinating and since it was useless to ask his temporarily deaf friend he sat and watched too.

As Foggy's tail swished she accidentally knocked a millipede from its cool, damp, mossy stone.

"Oh goodness gracious!" he groaned as he stretched out and checked that all his legs were still attached to his tiny body for he had been asleep. The Millipede trundled off underneath the stone mumbling about his rude awakening and tutting. After a heavy sigh he coiled himself up and was soon asleep none the worse for his experience.

Bracken yawned and lay down beside Foggy. There was something relaxing about watching this old beetle he decided. Now Foggy's eyes widened as a smaller, much faster beetle joined the large one.

"Any gossip Mr Beetle?" asked the large beetle with a twinkle in her eye.

"Gossip… gossip? Never gossiped in my life ma'am". He said unconvincingly. The old beetle chuckled when he smiled shrewdly and continued…

"Although… I did hear that Gossamer the rabbit kitten and Rufous the fox cub didn't return home last night. They were caught playing together the day before and scolded you know…."

"Well Mr Beetle I'm not surprised, it's not the done thing for a rabbit kitten to be playing with a fox cub…. Whatever is the world coming to…. But they're back home now?"

"Oh no, they're missing."

"Missing!…." cried the poor old beetle nearly falling off her wobbly legs. "… My dear fellow whatever do you mean?"

The animals meet the Boggart

15

"Aye. I flew to the farm today and over heard Tweed the Sheepdog making enquiries. Apparently Rufous's father asked Tweed for help to find his young'un and Tweed agreed so long as the old fox kept off his chickens".

"Oh very wise… very wise…. Poor wee ones. Mr Beetle, be a dear and help an old 'un up that hill. My legs don't work like they used to and my poor old wings are too brittle to fly…. Ah those were the days. I was quite a flyer in my day you know." She chuckled. Then her thoughts turned back to Gossamer and Rufous who were missing and she felt so sorry.

"Oh dear Mr Beetle, whatever shall be done? Oh dear, oh dear" Mr Beetle took her arm and smiled warmly at her.

Foggy and Bracken watched the beetles disappear into a ferny dell until the last 'Oh dear' was so faint Foggy had to strain her ears to hear it. Suddenly the blackbirds began to dive bomb Foggy because she was a cat and most cats hunt birds and these birds had a nest nearby.

"Come my dear," said Bracken gently nudging her with his nose. Foggy tutted, put her nose and tail up and marched off with her loyal friend.

"Oh." sighed Foggy so sadly it made Bracken whine too.

"I wish we could find Gossamer and Rufous", she said.

"And so we shall." Bracken replied decidedly.

"How?" Foggy asked frowning.

"First we need a search party," he announced.

"Oh yes, oh yes, let's send for our friends Jasper the tabby Cat and Grey the Squirrel. It's been ages since we saw them hasn't it Bracken?"

"Aye…hmmm…um…hmmmm." he said thinking.

Foggy's ears went down again.

"Oh no, what is it now?" she asked gingerly, half afraid of the answer.

"Well, they live miles away Foggy how will we get word to them?"

There was silence for neither of them had the answer. After a while it was decided to visit Tweed the Sheepdog to ask his advice and see if there was any news.

They walked briskly down Sandy Lane for quite some time and eventually came to a farm.

"Wait here, there may be other dogs beside." Bracken told Foggy. She gulped and hid in the hedge promising to wait.

"Cronk! Cronk! Cronk!" cried a raven from somewhere.

Bracken crept into the farmyard gingerly peering around a rustic old barn. Suddenly the chickens caught sight of him and on deciding he was a fox rather than a dog they panicked.

"Cluck! Cluck! Cluck! Ber Geer Buck Cluck!" they all cried flapping about with feather flying everywhere. Tweed rushed to the aid of the chickens thinking a fox had broken in and was relieved to find his old collie friend Bracken.

"Come!" yelled Bracken who suddenly caught sight of the nearing silhouette of the farmer with his rifle. Dashing off to Foggy's hiding place, Foggy wanted to know if they were playing sardines because she'd never been so squashed in her life!

As it turned out Tweed had no more information on the missing youngsters despite having searched all night long for clues. It seemed a hopeless situation but they sat chatting for a minute or two anyway.

"Tweed! Tweed!" yelled the farmer.

"It's no good, I've got to go." Tweed said getting up.

"Wait!" cried Foggy.

Tweed looked over his shoulder.

"We need to form a search party, will you join us?" pleaded Foggy.

"I'd give anything to help you but I can't leave the farm. My farmer friend needs me missy," he said.

"Then can you at least advise us how we can contact Jasper and Grey so they can come and help us?" asked Bracken.

"Aye, that's easy to do…"

"Tweeeeeed!!!" yelled a red faced farmer at the top of his voice.

"Leave it with me," called Tweed who began to yowl and yelp like a fox.

"Whatever is he doing?" said Foggy out of the corner of her mouth to Bracken.

"Saving himself trouble, clever stuff," replied Bracken who caught on immediately to Tweeds' game.

Tweed continued to play at being fox and Bracken snarled and barked so violently that Foggy shot off up the nearest tree. This went on for a while until Tweed rolled in the dirt and ran off to the farmer who made a fuss of him for chasing 'the fox' away that had supposedly startled his chickens.

"Huh!" said Foggy who joined Bracken again and together they wandered off back down Sandy Lane.

"Cronk! Cronk! Cronk!" said the raven hopping along behind them. They turned around.

"Well she's too big to catch." Whispered Foggy sarcastically for she was still annoyed at being frightened up the tree.

"Foggy!" Exclaimed Bracken shocked.

"Cronk! Cronk! Cronk! Message please," said the raven.

Foggy was smiling again now. Now everything was going to be alright. The raven was a friend of Tweeds who would often act as look out while Tweed had a rest in return for a few scraps. The raven took the message from Bracken, taking to the air and circling three times before she got her bearings. Then off she flew repeating the message over and over so as not to forget it.

"Well, if she flies as fast as that Jasper and Grey should be with us by morning," said Foggy impressed.

The night was drawing near but Foggy and Bracken did not rest. Instead they agreed to meet on the beach before morning and search the Burrows until their feet were sore. They split up so as to be able to cover a wider area. Bracken went to Ramshorn Pond where the lovely reeds were home to reed buntings and other creatures. Sniffing about, he was enchanted by the celery leaved buttercups and the pretty reflections they made in the water. Tiredness overcame him and he began to daydream when a startled frog leaped out of the water and was joined by two others.

"Croak", said the frog.

"Have you seen a rabbit kitten and a fox cub about here lately?" asked Bracken hopefully.

"Croak nope, croak nope, croak nope!" said the frogs plopping back into the water one after another.

"Huh! How about that!" exclaimed Bracken.

Meanwhile, Foggy was on another part of the Burrows patting the ground in a pitter-patter rhythm to bring the worms up so she could talk to them. After a while she overheard the following conversation.

"Is that rain Willaworma?"

"I'm not sure Wormelia!"

"Well we'd better rise to the surface just in case. I don't want to drown!"

"No… Wait! It may be a blackbird playing a trick!"

"Oh my!"

"Quick! Sing the peace song!"

Foggy heard them both clear their throats and sing….

"If you are a blackbird
I'm no worm
I'm just a stick
That learnt how to squirm"

"So if you are a blackbird
You can't eat me
For I am just a stick
And wont taste nice for tea".

Willaworma and Wormelia would not come to the surface whatever Foggy tried. She called to them but they fell silent… And so Foggy was forced to move on for time was of the essence.

Bracken and Foggy had searched the Burrows all night without finding a single clue as to the whereabouts of Rufous and Gossamer. Reluctantly both weary animals met up on the beach as agreed. Too tired to speak they both raised eyebrows hopefully and shook their heads sadly before flopping down to sleep on the soft sand.

Foggy and Bracken slept peacefully on the beach as the sun rose slowly. The water lapped around their feet bringing strange but peaceful dreams.

Meanwhile, somewhere in the distant sand dunes echoed two excited voices. A grey squirrel bounded through the marram grass and by his side was Jasper the Tabby Cat.

"Oh, an adventure! This is going to be so exciting!" Cried Grey the Squirrel.

After a while, they came to a huge sand dune and both animals decided it would be a good idea to reach the top to see what they could see. On the first attempt both reached half way and tumbled to the bottom laughing, but on the second attempt, and with the help of the marram grass, both reached the top safely. They could see for miles around. Jasper smiled and his eyes lit up as he exclaimed….

"There they are, asleep on the beach. I said they'd be there didn't I?"

"Oh well done! Now let's surprise them," cried Grey joyfully.

Within five minutes Jasper and Grey had reached the beach, but when they approached their sleeping friends, Bracken was snoring so loudly that Grey couldn't make himself heard. Jasper patted Foggy's tail playfully and sniffed her gently on the nose to which she opened one sleepy eye, yawned 'hooray!' and both cats curled up and fell asleep. Poor Grey squirrel on the other hand was so tired from their long walk he could barely put one paw in front of the other. Finding the soft warmth of Bracken's dense coat he walked into him with eyes already shut, flicked his tail over himself like a huge blanket and was asleep before his head had even touched the soft sandy ground. Bracken wagged his tail in his sleep knowing his friends had arrived.

The sun reached the highest point in the sky before the animals stirred. They rubbed their eyes, yawned, stretched and chatted excitedly. Walking inland, whilst deciding what to do next, they came across an ancient hawthorn tree that was gnarled and twisted by the harsh elements. It was surrounded by a huge toadstool ring that was still glistening from the early morning dew. The hawthorn tree was covered in the prettiest of lichens, and the animals felt an overwhelming sensation of peace here. Yet, the tree grew away from the buckthorn and other trees and shrubs. Strange how Bracken couldn't remember seeing it here before, especially when he thought he knew this place so well.

The creamy blossoms hung heavily on the tree and the animals decided this would be a good place to sit and plan their search for Rufous and Gossamer. Little did they know the tree was magical for it blossomed out of season. As they chatted, a tinkling sound of bells seemed to come from the tree and it shook slightly despite there being no wind. A strange mist swirled around the trunk and eventually enveloped the little party.

"Oh my!…. Are you there?" shouted Foggy, suddenly afraid because she couldn't see anyone.

"We're all here… but nobody must wander off for we shall lose each other for sure". Bracken commanded.

And the animals shouted 'Aye' in total agreement.

Suddenly the mist lifted to reveal the familiar surroundings once again, only, all the colours were so much brighter. The animals blinked, rubbed their eyes and blinked again.

"Everything's been painted by fairies!" said a startled but happy Grey squirrel.

There sounded laughter like silvery bells that filled the air and the animals hearts with joy.

"We have been watching you." said a silvery voice.

"Who said that?" asked Bracken looking up into the tree.

"I did", said the voice followed by a lot of giggling.

"May we join you?" asked another voice.

"Oh yes, please do." Foggy said who was quite intrigued.

The atmosphere was electrical yet good and no-one felt at all apprehensive about inviting their mysterious guests. Suddenly on a twinkling beam of stardust, which was every colour imaginable, The Queen of Faerie joined the animals while her people sat up in the tree.

"How lovely," said Grey enchanted by The Little People, for he had only ever read about them. They were far lovelier than any words or pictures he thought.

One fairy flew down and put a blossom on his head and of course being a squirrel Grey tried to eat it.

"I have been watching you in your endeavours to find Gossamer and Rufous," said the Queen continuing…. "I must tell you we suspect foul play but that is all I can tell you for now this is a battle which must be won".

Foggy gasped and the animals could hardly believe their ears.

"Foul play?" cried Jasper.

"Aye little one but I will protect you all by my powers and the powers of my people."

"And you can't tell us more?" asked Foggy.

"No because rules are rules and you must learn to follow your instincts and not let your emotions get the better of you," said the Queen softly.

"What should we do?" asked Bracken.

"You're doing very well and will do well for I have seen it. I will give you each a gift from my people. If you use your gifts wisely you will succeed." Said the Queen who promptly vanished with her people and the animals were seemingly alone once more.

Between Bracken and Foggy's paws was a small bunch of plants. Foggy was given the lovely yellow flowers of St. John's Wort, and Bracken was given a tiny fern called Moonwort. Jasper was given a large piece of gold stone and Grey had a smaller piece, probably because he wouldn't be able to carry anything larger. Puzzled the animals carefully carried their gifts and moved on together after thanking the Queen of Faerie.

Their next stop was at a small, concealed pond.

"This must be Doughnut Pond", said Bracken.

"Oh do let's stop and rest, my gold is heavy!" exclaimed Grey.

"Gold!!!" cried a voice and everyone looked round but there was no-one to be seen.

Bracken felt his hackles rise. Foggy noticed and became wary. Then they noticed a slight movement. What looked like a mushroom top with a cows tail on it, lifted and underneath a beady eyed Boggart peered at them.

"Did you say gold?" He asked innocently.

"Aye," said Grey "Why?"

The Boggart leapt up, threw his coracle, a small circular boat, into the pond and jumped in.

"Oh I just wondered," He said lounging in his boat looking at his nails.

"I don't suppose you've seen a rabbit kitten and a fox cub around here lately have you?" asked Bracken seizing the opportunity.

"What if I have… What's it worth?" asked the Boggart cunningly.

"My gold", said Grey.

"And mine!" said Jasper excitedly.

"No!…" Said Bracken raising his paw as the Boggart rubbed his hands together greedily.

"Grey's gold only, you might lie. You can earn the other piece later perhaps."

"I've never lied in my life!" Exclaimed the Boggart unconvincingly.

"Even so that is our unanimous decision." Bracken said firmly.

"Oh very well. Yes I have, now give me my gold." He said.

"Not until you tell us when you saw them and where they are now," Grey cut in before Bracken could speak.

The Boggart scratched his head, crossed his legs and arms fidgeting uncomfortably.

"Well?" said Bracken raising his eyebrows.

"Hmmmm…. Alright, they were here," he admitted.

"When?" asked Bracken.

"Night before last".

"Why?" asked Foggy.

"I promised them a ride in my coracle," replied the Boggart pointing down into his circular little boat.

The animals fell silent for a minute for they were astonished.

"What's your name?" asked Bracken through gritted teeth.

"Mandrake… why?"

Bracken felt a chill run through his stomach for he had heard about Mandrake and his awkward ways. He didn't answer the 'why' but went on to ask…

"Where did you take them Mandrake?"

"Hmmm… I've already earned my part of the bargain, now give me my gold!" He said fidgeting sulkily.

"Very well but if you take us to Gossamer and Rufous, Jasper will give you his gold as well," announced Grey and the animals nodded in approval.

Grey put the nugget into Mandrake's sweaty hand and it was snatched away rudely.

"Mine!" he cried triumphantly.

Grey's little face dropped and Foggy put her paw around him.

"Never mind dear, I'm sure you did the right thing," she whispered warmly. He nodded sadly and nuzzled into her.

"Now Mandrake!…. earn the other piece!" demanded Bracken.

Mandrake squinted at him for he did not like to be bossed about but, the other piece of gold was larger after all…

"Then get in," Said Mandrake smiling with his mouth but not with his eyes as he slyly pointed down into his coracle.

The mist swept in across the Burrows and everyone was suddenly enveloped in the dense white veil. It was like being in a strange dream despite the fact the animals knew their adventure was dangerously real. The mist grew thicker and the animals felt far wetter in the mist than they would have been in proper rain. Their strange companion took them across the pond but Bracken never once took his eyes off Mandrake for he knew he could not be trusted. Suddenly the coracle was spinning uncontrollably and they seemed to vanish into another realm behind the mist. There before them stood an ancient chapel half buried in the sand dunes. Gossamer and Rufous were inside but they could not get out.

"What have you done Mandrake!" Bracken barked.

Mandrake shrieked with laughter.

"Give me gold for you promised I should have it if I took you to Rufous and Gossamer and you can not go back on your word!" Shouted Mandrake and before Jasper could do anything about it Mandrake snatched the gold and vanished in his coracle leaving them all seemingly stranded.

Bracken began to dig away the sand around the chapel but it was useless for the marram grass roots had magically knitted together and were inseparable Next each animal put its tail through the chapel window to try to reach the youngsters but it was no good for no ones tail was long enough to reach them. Mandrake's laughter echoed through the air at each failed attempt.

"He's still here!" Foggy cried. Then she remembered her gift of St. John's Wort! She threw the bunch of yellow flowers through the window of the chapel knowing the flowers would protect against evil forces. There was a loud crack followed by a rumble of thunder in the air.

"Curses!" cried Mandrake suddenly afraid.

Bracken suddenly found the sand was coming away as he dug and eventually they found a door.

"It's no good, it's locked!" Grey sighed.

Bracken pushed the Moonwort Fern into the lock knowing that in folklore Moonwort unlocks doors and since the chapel was under Mandrake's spell, it worked. Foggy and Jasper leapt into the chapel.

"Don't be afraid, we're coming to take you home!" Jasper shouted bravely.

"Oh my, oh my!" Gossamer wailed crying with relief.

"We thought we'd be in here forever!" Rufous exclaimed as Jasper picked him up by the scruff of his neck.

"Are you alright little ones?" Foggy asked softly as she retrieved Gossamer who was trembling in the corner.

"I'm alright now!" said Rufous.

"But I'm afraid!" wailed Gossamer.

"Don't worry everything will be just fine." Foggy said.

Mandrake could be heard ranting and raving fiercely. The Queen of Faerie arrived on a beautiful silvery white unicorn. She threw something into the air and Mandrake was visible again. This annoyed him even more.

"Do as you will… " he said boldly "… for I have my gold!"

The Queen tossed back her head and laughed heartily.

"Foolsgold!" She declared pointing at the golden rock.

"It isn't real?" he asked weakly suddenly fearing her power.

"Of course not." she replied and continued…

"What possessed you to capture Gossamer and Rufous?"

"I was lonely Your Majesty…. And I…." He squirmed and fidgeted trying to find a good excuse for his prank but The Queen saw through him.

"You were bored more like!" she declared but he couldn't answer her.

"I'm sorry Your Majesty," he said weakly.

"Not truly you're not. You're only sorry because I will punish you," she said. Mandrake twiddled his thumbs.

"Your punishment is this….. You will spend the rest of your days doing tasks on the farm and doing them well. You will help Tweed the sheepdog while the Raven goes off to nest and you will do anything he tells you to do. And if you play pranks you will pay for them…. I will be watching you! Never forget!" Declared the Queen pointing at him and as Mandrake blinked the next moment he opened his eyes he was on the farm face to face with Tweed and Rufous's father.

As for the lost chapel, it became lost again to all but Faerie who transformed it into a beautiful Faerie Palace somewhere behind the veil. Jasper and Foggy were given an extra nine lives, Grey was given an endless resource of hazel nuts and Bracken was given the magical sycamore key to the Faerie palace which appears once a year on Midsummer's Eve… and so it was that the animals learnt that goodness always wins in the end.

As it happens, Mandrake works surprisingly well and loves the farm life. He has become a sort of house-sprite, living round and about the old farmhouse and the farmland, helping the animals and the farmer at Tweeds command. Of course the farmer cannot see him, he thinks his wife has completed a task and his wife thinks her husband has done it. So Mandrake is far too busy to be bored but he is also very happy. As for the animals, they will rest and reap their rewards until perhaps another adventure comes their way.

THE END

The Adventures of Timothy

P.C. Timothy Truncheon on Castle Mound

Down along the River Taw lies an old market town known as Barnstaple. Its population has expanded gradually over the years with improvements to the town being made every so often yet Castle Mound has survived in the heart of the town with its gently winding path leading to the top. The Normans had built the huge mound of soil 900 years ago as a motte and bailey lookout point.

In the summer, the lush foliage of the tree canopies reveal the shape of Castle Mound and beneath the dappled shadows a habitat for many wild flowers, birds and small mammals. Situated opposite the Police Station in Castle Green, the people of Barnstaple bustle about their everyday business. Yet, little do they know the adventures that go on in Castle Mound for it is the home of Timothy Truncheon the Police-Mouse.

P.C. Timothy Truncheon is an extremely hard working little fellow. Being a mouse he sleeps for four hours and then works for four hours, so he is on the beat day and night, and manages all the shift work needed to keep the creatures of Castle Mound in check.

It is 3 o'clock in the afternoon and Timothy is fast asleep. One can usually tell if he is home because whilst he is generally very quiet, he has a tendency to talk in his sleep. He says things like "Gotcha!" and "Thought you'd out smart me eh!" and things like that.

Now it just so happened that Miss Tilly Mouse, who lives in Hazel Thicket on the other side of the Mound, was bustling along inspecting grass seeds and deciding they weren't quite ready for harvesting, when all of a sudden a terrible panic attack swept over her as five hairy bearded faces appeared before her on the wing. Robber Flies! They flew all about her asking her all sorts of questions such as where they might find the Dor Beetle's house, who he hangs out with, and where he goes. Well, poor Miss Tilly Mouse was so afraid all she could do was squeak unintelligibly. One Robber Fly shouted at her to answer the questions and called her a 'country bumpkin', which fortunately roused P.C. Timothy Truncheon from his slumber. In seconds he scampered onto the scene demanding to know what was going on. Seeing Miss Tilly Mouse's distress he waved his truncheon furiously at the Robber Flies and demanded they be gone. One fly rubbed his funny beard, another pulled a quirky face, which made another laugh and poke his tongue out. The remaining two flies merely stared blankly and before you could even blink, the whole band vanished buzzing irritably. Then there was peace. Miss Tilly Mouse was so shaken that P.C. Truncheon guided her back home to her cosy mouse-hole where he made her a strong cup of nettle tea in her favourite little acorn cups.

"Why did the Robber Flies want to know where the Dor Beetle lived?" Asked Tilly

"Well, Robber Flies eat insects, after first injecting them with poison. There's something rather more sinister with this band though. I think they're from M.I. 7. If I'm right then they are looking for traitors." P.C. Truncheon sighed.

"Is the Dor Beetle a traitor then?" gasped Miss Tilly Mouse.

"Not as far as I know, though I believe he has done a lot of undercover work for the Government. If his cover has been blown, well, they may have been sent to eat him but I sincerely hope not." replied P.C. Truncheon in a low tone.

"Oh my!" squeaked Tilly but P.C. Truncheon assured her…

"Don't worry miss, I'll pay the Dor Beetle a visit and get to the bottom of all this."

So that same afternoon, P.C. Truncheon pays Dorbie the Dor Beetle a visit. As soon as Dorbie learns about the Robber Flies he becomes terribly nervous and can't help stuttering 'Oh my' all the time. Well Timothy is immediately suspicious. Why is Dorbie so afraid? What has he done? Something is definitely afoot he decides.

"I can't possibly help you Dorbie unless you tell me the absolute truth and nothing but the truth." said P.C. Truncheon firmly with a frown.

Castle Mound

*Timothy & Tilly Mice meet
Dorbie the Dor Beetle*

There was an uncomfortable pause before Dorbie decided to speak.

"Well, it all happened like this Constable Truncheon….." began Dorbie pausing for thought and continuing…

"I was up at White Hole in London having finished my final assignment. We all went to the High Flyers club in Antenna Street for lunch to celebrate. There I was presented with a book as a retirement gift." Dorbie fetched a green book bound in hazel leaves and written with genuine squid ink. The leaf cutter bees had done a superb job in binding the book and the pages were glued in with a special honey made for the job.

"A beautiful gift." P.C. Truncheon mumbled as he inspected the book obviously impressed as Dorbie went on with his story.

"Well after lunch we were all feeling pretty good. I picked up my book, took a leisurely snail ride through the park with a few friends before winging my way back here."

"Hmm… nothing odd so far carry on." P.C. Truncheon encouraged.

"Well, it had been a long day so I went to bed and slept as snug as a bug in a rug. It wasn't until the Robin brought me a parcel in the early morning post, yesterday, I'd realised something was terribly wrong." Dorbie wiped away a tear from his eye and his funny little legs began to shake as he tried to explain….

"I'd picked up the wrong book! My book arrived in the post, after having apparently forgotten to take it home but this one is almost identical. See here…" Dorbie handed a second book to P.C. Truncheon to examine.

"I say!" P.C. Truncheon exclaimed. "Do you know what this is?"

"I'm afraid I do. It is the official book of every Secret Agent in the country. Now it's too late and M.I. 7 think I'm a traitor, a double agent. They're going to kill me aren't they?" wailed the poor Dor Beetle as he wiped sweat from his brow in his despair.

P.C. Truncheon was thinking. They both sipped iced nettle tea and finding it most refreshing P.C. Truncheon began to feel an idea forming in the back of his mind. He sends

Commander Owl

for a Blue Tit. Blue Tit kindly takes a message to Miss Tilly Mouse and to the Tawny Owl to meet P.C. Truncheon on official police business. Merely seconds after concluding this business, the Robber Flies are back!

Dorbie ambled along with the "Forbidden Book of Named Agents" with the intention of being extremely brave and giving it back to the Robber Flies so they can return it to White Hole whatever the consequences. However, the Robber Flies spot him instantly and armed with their poison make sudden dash for Dorbie. P.C. Truncheon has to think quickly if he's going to save the old beetle. He elbows Dorbie, who goes tumbling down a mud-slide that the rabbits had made in their games. Dorbie looses his grip on the book as he hurtles down, down, down.

Meanwhile Miss Tilly Mouse and The Tawny Owl are in position. Out of the early evening shadows comes Tilly just in time to grab Dorbie's back legs and pull him to safety into her own mouse-hole dwelling. She gives a loud squeak and suddenly the tawny owl arrives on the scene to land by the book to ensure it does not go astray again. Now the Robber Flies have arrived at the bottom of the mud-slide to find owl licking his beak and the book safe by his side. And so it was that the Robber Flies retrieved the "Forbidden Book of Secret Agents", assumed owl had eaten Dorbie the Dor Beetle and were soon winging their way back to White Hole.

Now, all they had to do was to move Dorbie into a new home, leaving his old home intact as though the occupant really had died suddenly. Miss Tilly Mouse decided that they should change Dorbie's appearance for good measure but how on earth do you change a Dor Beetle's appearance! Well, Tilly certainly came up with the answer. She curled his antennae! Now Dorbie looks very handsome for an old boy. He even changed his name to Dor the Dor Beetle. Now the old beetle feels safe, thanks to his friends.

The night air is chilly and P.C. Timothy Truncheon has to file a report. So it's back to Mouse-Hole Station to get on with the job. When he arrives at his desk however, there is a surprise indeed - a promotion to Sergeant. Heavens! Little did Timothy know that the owl he'd asked for help during the evening's events was non other than Commander Owl of the Metropolitan Animal Police Force. So it's hooray for Sergeant Timothy Truncheon. He gets three cheers from all the animals of Castle Mound. Oh how proud he feels.

THE END

Miss Tilly Mouse has a Bad Day

Night-time fell on Castle Mound. All the creatures that lived there slept save for owls and other creatures of the night. The full moon cast tree shadows upon Castle Green beneath the old Holm Oak. This tree never lost its leaves during autumn and winter-time as it was ever-green. So now, only the lovely Holm Oak's leaves glistened in the light rain that fell like jewels upon its leaves and the spider's webs that sparkled in the moonlight amongst the bramble. For that moment, had anyone been walking by at that hour, they would have been forgiven for believing diamonds lay amongst the webs that billowed in the softest of breezes.

What peace and tranquillity, if only it could have lasted forever but, alas it was soon to be broken. Two weasels fought viciously in the darkness, screaming like banshees, over a territorial dispute. Sgt Timothy Truncheon heard it but was powerless to do anything unless three complaints were filed.

The first to complain was the dormouse. He'd headed straight to Mouse-Hole Station with the knowledge day-break was close and he needed sleep having been active all night long. P.C. Truncheon filed his complaint and so the grumbling dormouse headed back to his hazel tree shelter and not all that far from Miss Tilly Mouse's House, in a most perplexed mood. Sure enough Miss Tilly Mouse came next.

"Oh P.C. Truncheon, can't you do something the noise is just awful!" pleaded Miss Tilly Mouse.

P.C. Truncheon filed the second complaint. In the following few moments Shrew, Bank Vole and Owl also complained and P.C. Truncheon had to write very fast in order to keep up because everyone was talking at the same time. Had you been there I'm sure you would have observed steam coming from his charcoal pencil!

Owl complained that the sound of weasels fighting frightened away his prey. He was furiously angry at having his night hunting spoiled. Miss Tilly Mouse insisted that 'the noise was awfully offensive' and Bank Vole and Shrew were too afraid to say very much at all.

So there it was. There was in fact nothing for it but to arrest and lock up the two weasels on the grounds of disturbing the peace. Now had it not been for Timothy's truncheon, which always hung at his side, the weasels would have certainly caught and eaten this brave little Police-mouse. It was a risky business, arresting weasels. P.C. Truncheon was brave but he managed to hold them for several hours, until they had calmed down. He then sent them packing with a caution saying he hoped they'd learnt their lesson.

As soon as peace reigned again, Miss Tilly Mouse was screaming "Help, Help, Help!" An owl was after her and in her panic she was suddenly disorientated and couldn't find her way home. Since Commander Owl of the Metropolitan Animal Police Force was away in London, another owl had invaded his territory in his absence deciding that poor Miss Tilly Mouse would make an awfully tasty morsel! P.C. Truncheon only just managed to yank Tilly Mouse out of the owls reach just in the nick of time. She even felt the dreadful 'whooooosh' of the owl's talons pass by her.

"Now that's the second time we've met tonight Miss Tilly Mouse mam." Sgt Truncheon grinned at her.

"Oh, yes indeed, so sorry." Miss Tilly Mouse blushed, scampering away before anything else could happen, but oh, too late. In her haste she stumbled and tripped over a tangle of

P.C. Timothy Truncheon rounds up the culprits

ivy. She heard the 'tut' of a Brimstone butterfly that was trying to find a place to hibernate there and fell flat on her little nose. Bomp!

"Oh dear, it's not my night tonight is it!" She wailed.

Luckily dawn was now breaking and the owl had gone home to roost. Blue Tit awoke to find poor Miss Tilly Mouse rubbing her ankle, which she had twisted badly. It was too painful to take her weight, light as she was. Blue Tit flew straight to Mouse-Hole Station twittering rapidly the news of Miss Tilly Mouse and her poorly ankle. Sgt Truncheon marched straight off to rescue her once again. By the time he arrived on the scene Tilly was able to hobble just a little and with Sgt Truncheon's help she managed to get back to her own cosy little house in Hazel Thicket. Everything was golden lit as the sun began to rise. It was really quite beautiful. She assured Sgt Truncheon that she didn't need anything and was quite alright. She wanted only to go to bed having had quite enough for one day, even though it had only just begun, for the weasels had kept her awake for most of the night. She was simply exhausted and went promptly to bed falling to sleep the instant her furry head touched her mossy pillow. She had a disturbed sleep unsettled in thinking she had forgotten something. What was it… oh!

As the day grew warmer with the rising of the sun, Robin finished his animal post round and was heading back to his favourite singing post when he found a package containing berries, nuts and grass seeds, obviously collected for someone's winter cache. Like a good Robin he turned the cache over to the police.

As Sgt Timothy Truncheon inspected the package thoroughly he found it to have no name or address. There was only one thing for it. He'd have to send it off to forensics to test for paw prints. It was all in hand or shall we say 'in paw'. He'd know late that same afternoon whose parcel it was the minute the results came through. He was an efficient Police-mouse.

Somehow it was no surprise to him that the Paw Prints identified belonged to Miss Tilly Mouse.

"Not again!" He sighed, deciding it must be fate taking a hand.

Sgt Timothy Truncheon scuttled off to Hazel Thicket. Luckily Tilly was at home. She was overjoyed to be reunited with her package, which she had dropped in all the commotion of

Timothy & Tilly

her previous adventures. She was sure she had forgotten something but couldn't put her finger on it. What a relief to have it back. Thankfully after her rest she was quite herself again now.

"It's no good Miss Tilly Mouse you'll just have to marry me. That way I can keep an eye on you." teased Sgt Truncheon.

Well, Tilly blushed most profusely.

"Perhaps in spring." she teased him back.

Now it was his turn to blush. Who knows, perhaps they will marry in the spring for they would make a handsome couple. For now, it's just the end of another adventure on Castle Mound in the heart of Barnstaple.

THE END

The Adventures of Willow

Willow the Magic Moon Dog

Old Midsummer's Eve had been a beautiful day. St. John's Wort flowers had burst open to reveal splendid small golden petals, so pretty amongst the pink Century flowers, the deep blood red of Hedge Woundwort and many others. Macracken Farm near Woody Bay was a picture at this time of year. Hazel, the much trusted sheepdog, was heavy with young and unable to work. How tired and restless she felt today. The farmer Pat, a big burly man, took great pride in Hazel for she was wonderful with the sheep, so patient and calm.

"If they pups be anythin' like our 'azel, us wont go far wrong." Mused Pat to his wife in his broad Devonshire accent.

The farmer's wife Susan, was looking forward to their new project for she was going to be in charge of training the puppies, once they were old enough, to be good sheepdogs like their mum. She'd trained Hazel herself years ago and seemed to have a real flair for it. Once during the popular television show "One Man & His Dog", Susan had said to her husband,

"Look dear, that could be us with our Hazel." She'd meant to tease her husband but a warm light sparked in his eyes and so began the beginning of a dream project. Now that dream would soon become a reality with the coming of Hazel's puppies.

So that night, Hazel wandered off alone. She wanted the peace and solitude of the old barn. The night was still, dry and overcast but it was not cold. Before midnight Hazel had given birth to four healthy puppies. Susan looked in every so often to make sure all was well since this was Hazel's first litter. Susan and Pat were anxious for Hazel and they weren't going to abandon their loyal friend in her time of need. Susan heard their Grandfather Clock strike Midnight. The cloud seemed to break and a silvery moonbeam streamed through the barn window to touch Hazel. Susan thought how pretty Hazel looked with her puppies when suddenly Hazel had one more puppy, so now there were five. This fifth puppy was smaller than the others but it was breathing and all seemed well. Susan must have been feeling extremely tired for she could have sworn she saw a fairy dancing in the moon beam and casting star dust on the last puppy. It was an enchanting sight and took Susan's breath away. She rubbed her eyes and the vision was gone, along with the moonbeam.

As the weeks went by eventually the puppies eye's opened and slowly they began to grow proper coats like their mum. The smallest puppy however, did not resemble the others for he was all white with two big black butterfly-like ears and freckles on his nose, whereas the other little dogs had the 'traditional black bodies with white markings of proper collie dogs' as Pat bluntly put it to his wife one day. Pat wanted to give him away but Susan wouldn't hear of it. Luckily Susan had a soft spot for this 'odd' little puppy for his warm brown eyes melted her heart and she felt he needed her.

A year later saw an extremely happy family of sheepdogs, all keen and bright eyed. Hazel was so proud of her family. It was fantastic that they could all stay together and not be split up and sold, as with other farm dogs in the area when a litter arrived. Hazel had but one worry. The white bodied sheepdog Susan had named Willow, after the white willow that grew on their farm. Willow was terrified of sheep. Hazel had talked to him and encouraged him as best she could but to no avail. Eventually Willow confided in his mother that the old ewe was bad tempered and forever stamping her feet at him. Willow was totally convinced that the minute Susan's back was turned, that old ewe was going to head-but him into the next field.

"She seems to lead all the others, Mother. It isn't fair, Oak never has any trouble and Halse keeps calling me a 'chicken'. It just isn't fair. There must be something I'm good at!" Willow whimpered.

All Hazel could do was to lick his face and tell him all would be well. And so it was that Susan kept Willow as her pet and trained the other dogs for trials. Willow stayed with Susan in the farmhouse away from the working dogs unless they were all out together. Something in the back of Susan's mind told her that Willow was 'special' but she couldn't put her finger on it. It was something in her heart, a knowing and a feeling her husband did not share.

Of course as soon as the other young sheepdogs heard of Willow's privileged position, they started on him. Clearly Oak, was the top dog, the cleverest of the young sheepdogs whilst Halse and Guelder, his sisters, were not far behind. But Cob, the other brother, muddled along and often took his vexation out on Willow. Cob was forever barking at Willow and calling him 'bottom dog'. Hazel was extremely angry when she found out but there was not much she could do about it for Willow never complained and Hazel only ever found out if she caught Cob in the act. Poor Willow often whimpered in his sleep on the days he had been bullied. He suffered in silence.

One night the farmer put the sheepdogs, his pride and joy, to bed in the old barn early for a storm was brewing. The dogs were well fed and well exercised and they didn't mind in the least. They were never chained up in the barn and had free reign to play. Hazel kept an eye on any rough behaviour so all was well. Susan was taking cocoa for herself and for her husband upstairs to bed. Before she went she always kissed Willow on the head and watched him jump up on his blanket on the old sofa in the kitchen. The moment he was settled she'd quietly close the door smiling and that would be it for the night.

This night was different. Whether it was the storm that gave Willow a restless night or whether Cobs bullying had anything to do with it, he could not tell but Willow dreamed strangely. In his dream he saw a bright yellow van arrive at the gates and two rough looking men got out speaking low and gruffly. He watched them climb the large farm gates that Pat padlocked at six O'clock every night without fail, unless he was hay-making or some such. The men wore balaclavas and carried large cans of something liquid. They made for the sheepdog barn. Willow could hear his family barking and Oak's low growl. What was happening? What was going on? Who were these men? Willow saw the men splash about the liquid stuff, set it alight and vanish into the darkness. Willow wanted to wake from this awful dream, he kicked his legs in his sleep and whimpered but he did not wake. He heard the whines and yelps of his beloved family as they were all killed in the ravishing fire. Suddenly he fell off his sofa and woke up. Thank goodness, only a dream….

It was dark outside and Willow had a long drink of water from his bowl. The storm had abated. It had been mostly wind with short bursts of rain and some lightning. Peace. Willow was alone in the silence. He wanted a hug from Susan. He listened to the clock gently ticking in the hallway but the kitchen door was shut. Then went to the back door and sniffed and listened. Straining his ears he could hear his brothers snoring gently so Willow felt better.

In the morning Willow ran straight to his mother to tell her of his dream. His brothers and sisters listened. He told them about the Yellow Van and the two men. Guelder said that a yellow van passed by from a neighbouring farm sometimes and Mother Hazel confirmed that. Halse said that she had heard dogs barking from that farm and wondered if they were training to be sheepdogs too. Then there was excitement in case the 'other' sheepdogs were going to the trials.

"Do you think we'll get to meet them?" Asked Guelder excitedly, for she wasn't a bit competitive.

"They'll be shame faced when I beat them all at the trials! Last time I went with the Master on my own I beat them then and I'll beat them again." Boasted Oak.

"Yeah!" Cob barked joining in with his brother.

"Now, now, you must show good sports-dog-ship and not let me be ashamed of you." Mother Hazel told them raising her eye-brows.

Then Willow came to the part of the dream where the old barn was set alight. Cob barked at Willow saying he was only jealous because he wasn't going to the trials. Oak pooh-poohed Willow's dream and then there came arguments and the usual bullying Willow always got.

"May be the other farmer doesn't want you for competition. Did you ever think of that!" Willow snapped.

Hazel had to calm them all down, although she was secretly proud of Willow for sticking up for himself, but also concerned for he was a good dog and did not make up stories.

The following evening saw the usual routine of locking up gates, putting the chickens to bed, checking the sheep one last time and putting the working dogs in the old barn for the night. The key turned in the old kitchen door that must have been a hundred years old, and Susan put Pat's super on the table. It was a peaceful evening with lovely skies as the sun set. Willow loved gazing out of the windows watching the rabbits playing in the field.

That night Willow couldn't settle at all. Susan left Willow on the sofa in the large country kitchen and went off to bed as usual. Willow's sleep was broken for several hours. Finally there came the rumble of a vehicle drawing up to the farm gates. Willow pricked his ears up and leaped from the sofa to the low window over-looking the yard. It was a yellow van! Willow gave himself a good shake and bits of white fur floated about as he did so. No, it was definitely a yellow van and two men wearing balaclavas were climbing over the gate. Willow was so terrified he lost his bark for a moment. His dream had been a premonition! It was happening, actually happening. What could he do? He knew he'd have to think and act quickly.

Suddenly Willow found his bark so he barked with all his might. All the other dogs heard him, and they too began to bark but Pat shouted at Willow and told him to be quiet. The men were carrying a can containing something liquid and they were approaching the barn, faster now. A chill of dread ran down Willow's spine. He leaped at the kitchen door, which somehow jarred the latch open. With his paws and nose he nudged the old oak door open.

Luckily Pat kept the hinges well oiled so Willow didn't have too much trouble. Next he bolted up the stairs to bark and whine outside the bedroom door of his Master and Mistress. Now Pat and Susan knew something was wrong for Willow may have been useless as a sheepdog, but never was he disobedient. As quick as Susan was it was Pat that was first to the door, pulling on his dressing gown and slippers. Willow wandered back and forth coaxing Pat to follow him and licking his licks submissively.

"Stay here!" He told his wife, who was already dressing again. He was suddenly concerned. "Show me boy!" He urged.

Willow led Pat downstairs to the kitchen door. Pat and Willow were soon in the Yard and the intruders were spotted. Pat couldn't believe it. With an open mouth he watched his neighbour's son splash and pour petrol all over his barn. Pat ran as fast as he could and shouting at the top of his voice. He felt sure the culprits would run for it but no, they did not. Spike, the older brother, went for Pat grabbing his arms. Pat put up a struggle and defended himself well.

"What are you doing Spike! Let's run for it!" The younger man said.

"No mate it's too late, he'll snitch on us. Open the barn door." Ordered Spike through gritted teeth.

Willow nipped Spike's elbow several times. He was not a vicious dog but he wanted to make Spike let go of his Master.

"Ah!" yelled Spike booting Willow out of the way.

"Let go of him brother or the dog will go for you!" yelled the younger one.

"Shut up Sam and do as I tell you."

Sam opened the barn door just enough to shove Pat in without the other dogs getting out. They tried to grab Willow but Willow was too quick and leaped about the yard making all the noise he could.

"Give me the matches." Snarled Spike at his brother.

"Spike no, no you can't, it's murder!" cried Sam.

"Given 'em to me!" snapped Spike grabbing the matches out of Sam's trembling hands. "I want no more competition from this lot. Our dogs are going to win the trials for once."

The next few moments seemed to happen in slow motion. The match struck the box. Then there was a flame, a bright flame. Then a 'whoosh' as it made contact with the petrol and the barn was suddenly alight. There was nothing Willow could do. He had wanted to stop these events, having dreamed of them the night before, but all he had done was effectively made everything worse. And so he howled. He howled with all his might. But then there was another howl, the howling of a siren and flashing lights. The police arrived. But how had they known? Fortunately Susan had phoned them the moment her husband had left. She happened to look out of the bedroom window to see the intruders. Now she was running, running to free her husband from the blazing barn. The police had warned her to remain where she was at least until they arrived.

Soon the criminals were handcuffed and a fire engine had come to help put out the blaze. Susan managed to open the barn door, for the police had been busy catching the criminals. Out staggered Pat with all the lovely sheepdogs, all unhurt but a little shaken. Down burnt the barn not a scrap of it could be saved. Susan threw her arms around her husband.

"Oh Pat, if it hadn't been for Willow…." Cried Susan as tears of relief ran down her face.

When Pat finally found his voice he turned to Willow and said rather shakily,

"I'm promoting you boy, to guard dog and top dog!" All the working dogs barked their approval, even Cob, and all was well.

The following week there was a write up in the paper about Willow being the bravest dog and receiving commendation from the police. Everyone was so proud but it didn't end there. Oak went on to win many Sheepdog Trials. His sisters Guelder and Halse worked well as a pair. They only ever won anything when they worked together but they were winners also. As for Cob, he watched in admiration and did his best. Maybe he'd win a trail one day for there was still plenty of time. Thankfully the insurance company paid for a new barn to be installed, which was far better than the old barn, to house the working sheepdogs. Mother Hazel was so very proud of her family, she really felt blessed. Even Cob secretly put Willow in his prayers at night. All the dogs held Willow in awe, especially his mother.

As for Willow himself, he went on to have many premonitions, not all as dramatic but some were. He once foresaw Susan in a terrible car crash that had badly injured her. It was one morning on her way to town as she descended the steep slope down into Lynmouth. Her brakes had given way and she hadn't been able to pull into one of the emergency lay-bys. Willow consulted his mother often when he was unsure what to do. She had come up with the idea of stuffing a potato in the exhaust pipe so that is exactly what they did. Willow had heard later over supper, as Susan had chatted to her husband, how the car had 'just stopped' a short way along on her journey to town. She called the AA on her mobile and was told she'd been extremely lucky because her brakes were also faulty. The car was due for its M.O.T. the following week!

Willow's many dreams were not all so dramatic. Sometimes he dreamed about sheep escaping through gaps in the boundary so he was able to lead Susan to them and watch Pat fix them before the livestock could break free. Best of all Willow was happy, really happy. If only Pat and Susan had known the truth about Willow. How amazed they would be.

One night however, Susan couldn't sleep. She came down into the kitchen for a glass of water. As she gingerly opened the kitchen door, for she was not sure whether Willow was perhaps asleep behind it. He was often there on the cool stone slabs when it was a hot night. She gazed across the room and there in a beautiful moonbeam lay Willow sound asleep. By his side a silvery voiced fairy whispered in his ear. Susan could not hear the words. The fairy looked up at Susan and smiled, then she curled up on Willow's back fluttering her shimmering wings and went to sleep.

"So I hadn't been mistaken." Said Susan to herself remembering the night Willow was born in the old barn as a fairy had danced in the moon beam to scatter star dust upon his tiny being. She hadn't dreamed it up at all. It was real.

Susan often saw the fairy after that riding on Willow's back or sleeping in his fur, but more than often whispering in his ear. Susan felt very privileged for her husband Pat never saw the fairy, though he would often comment that Willow was in a world of his own. And so began the legends of Willow the Magic Moon Dog that would be passed down to every sheepdog that was ever to be born on Macracken Farm.

"Good night, my lovely Magic Moon Dog." Susan whispered.

THE END

Willow & The Mouseketeers

By mid-spring the farmer and his wife were talking about the strange winds and erratic rainfall. "It's all this Climate Change business I reckon." gruffed Pat to his wife.

"Well I know one thing. The rain is all or nothing these days." replied Susan. Willow the white bodied sheepdog that had black butterfly-like ears and freckles on his nose, had remained on the farm as guard dog and as Susan's companion all these years. He heard his Master and Mistress discussing better ways of preserving water and how they'd saved a lot of money by going on a meter. Well, it was all as clear as mud to Willow because he didn't know what a meter was.

Macracken farm ran as an efficient business though Pat would often grumble at the amount of paperwork to do. It was true, farm related paperwork seemed to increase year by year as more restrictions and regulations became enforced.

"Weren't like it in my father's day." Pat would complain.

Susan would then cheer her hard working husband up by bringing him a piece of pie or something she had freshly baked. Pat always went quiet then, absorbed in the delicious taste and smell. Susan had begun selling farm produce in the market once a week. If she had a lot she would often take Willow along so he could guard the stall as Pat was busy on the farm most days. Willow enjoyed Market days, there were always so many interesting smells and then there were people bustling and gossip, always gossip. Willow would often cringe as old ladies would go on about this operation and that operation, but more interestingly he'd learn about life on other farms from the chatter of some of the farming neighbours.

Macracken Farm was successful. They now bred pedigree sheepdogs and Willow's brothers and sisters were all well known throughout the County and beyond. Oak never failed to win a sheepdog trial now when he took part, but their dear mother Hazel was now retired from her duties. This was better for Willow as he could talk to her more often and they had jolly times together. So life was relaxed and happy until one night….

It had been a full year since Willow had had one of his enchanted dreams but out of the blue he suddenly had one. Willow slept deeply when he dreamed, twitching his nose and whiskers. He made funny little noises in his sleep and his paws made running movements usually. His dream this time was strange and erratic. The dream began in a heat haze. Willow could feel the heat and remembered feeling so hot that he wished he'd been a sheep so he could have his coat shaved off. He saw his brothers rounding up the sheep, panting with strained effort. Vegetation was wilting and there in the hay meadows were little shadows silhouetted in the sunlight. What were they? Willow's dream took him closer, he seemed to float over the fields. Mice, they were mice, hundreds of them. Then he dreamed of mice in the kitchen running amok and mice in his bed. Ah too many mice!

Willow's dream seemed to reach a climax and then it faded. There before him stood a beautiful fairy in golden attire. Her silvery wings fluttered and she spoke to him.

"Willow, you can prevent this plague and save Susan's kitchen from being closed down by the authorities. She works so hard and keeps a good clean kitchen. She would never live down the humiliation. Imagine the gossip!" The fairy was shaking her head in thought and then continued.

"You must seek out and find the Mouseketeers. Bring them here so they can prevent this plague from happening. Be quick!" She said and then she was gone and Willow's dream ended.

Rascal the Mouseketeer leader

When Willow awoke, he went straight off to find his mother. Hazel listened intently.

"Sounds like cats to me. I've never been too fond of cats myself although old smudge is alright I suppose." Hazel mused. She told Willow to go and find the old farm cat and ask her if she had ever heard of the Mouseketeers. So Willow went off to find Smudge sleeping under a bush. Willow asked her if she'd ever heard of Mouseketeers.

"I think I have dear boy," began Smudge "I think they are cats that mouse. I wasn't too bad in my day you know but one gets old. Teeth aren't what they used to be." But Smudge didn't know where to find the Mouseketeers and advised him to ask his mother Hazel. Well, that wasn't much good because his mother had said to ask Smudge. So back to square one again. Willow told Hazel what Smudge had said and Hazel said,

"Well ask your father then."

Now Willow's father belonged to the duck egg lady in the Market. Market day was tomorrow so Willow hoped and prayed Susan would take him with her. She didn't always. It would be pot luck.

The next morning saw a lovely dawn followed by a fine day. Susan was loading her van with home baked produce, chicken eggs, honey and jam. She'd even made aprons, peg bags and lavender bags. Susan never could sit still, even in front of the television she'd be fiddling with something. Susan kissed her husband and went to climb in the van and Willow whined.

"You've never done that before Willow." Said Susan surprised.

Then smiling she told him, "Very well then, come." Her commands to the dogs were always simple words or whistles though Willow understood a far wider human vocabulary then the other dogs because he lived in the farmhouse as a non working dog.

Willow leapt up into the van and proudly sat next to his mistress as she drove off. It was still very early and when they got to market people were putting up trestle tables and yawning as they put their goods on show. The duck egg lady hadn't arrived and Willow began to wonder if she was coming today. Eventually she arrived in a fluster telling Susan that her husband had dropped his cooked breakfast all over the floor because he was out with the lads and didn't get in until late. Apparently he'd fallen asleep over breakfast and knocked the lot off the table.

"Took me a hour to get those devil-some stains out of my new carpet. And you should have seen the state of him. I tell you Susan I didn't know whether to laugh or cry! Eh I'll tell you one thing, the dog was happy because he ate the lot!" Said Gwen, the duck egg lady.

"Oh well Gwen, saved you having to pick it up then." Giggle Susan. She and Susan would have the giggles all day now.

Willow thought his father was looking rather pleased with himself. Well that explained it. He always did have a sharp eye for an opportunity.

"Morning Lad." said his father with a twinkle in his eye and settling down beneath one of the large trestle tables.

Willow settled along side his father and explained about his dream and how the fairy had urged him to find the Mousketeers. His father was thoughtful for a while and then he said:

"Well, I hope you know what you're getting yourself into boy. The head of the Mousketeers is a wild soul and goes by the name of Rascal. He'll want something if you put him to task, be sure of that. He's a Tabby Cat if I remember rightly. Hmm, get him on your side though and you wont go far wrong."

"But where can I find him father?" pleaded Willow urgently.

"Well now, there's the thing. I don't know. I should go and see old Mrs Crab in the village.

Her dog Meg will know for sure. There isn't a cat about that hasn't been chased by Meg." answered his father with a wily grin.

So there it was…. a new lead. Willow would wait until they reached home and as soon as Susan let Willow out. He'd leap the gate and go in search of Meg. My! How the rest of the day dragged.

"Willow you are a proper fidget today. Never mind we'll be away early today. I'll have sold everything by two O'clock the rate this lots going, but be still now." Susan told Willow rubbing his head. She thought he wouldn't understand that her voice would sooth him. Well, so it did but he also understood every word and so did Willow's father who was winking at him knowingly.

Finally they were trundling off in the van homeward bound. As Susan busied herself unloading the empty trays for washing, Willow dashed off. Seen by no-one he leaped the gate and was heading for the heart of Woody Bay to find Mrs Crab. Now, all the children were afraid of Mrs Crab because she had a funny temper. She also had little hair and few teeth but she was amazing with her knowledge of herbs and healing. Rumour has it she once healed a man's broken ankle in three weeks instead of the usual six and when doctors x-rayed the broken bones they could actually see the new bones knitting together and where the original break had been. Willow approached her cottage gingerly. Luckily Meg was asleep by the gate. She was a short haired scruffy little dog with a yappy bark but quite friendly.

"Who goes there, who goes there?" Yapped Meg waking up the moment she sensed Willow's presence.

"It is Willow, I…" But Meg interrupted.

"Do you want a potion, are you ill?" She asked hurriedly.

"No I…" Willow tried to answer but Meg interrupted.

"Ah well, then perhaps you have a bad paw?"

"No." Willow said.

"A bad leg then?" Meg persisted.

"No." Willow said.

"Which bit of you is bad then?" Asked Meg persistently.

"None of me. I'm very well thank you very much." Answered Willow.

"So why have you come then?"

"Well," said Willow waiting for her to interrupt him again but she didn't, "I've come for some advice if you please Meg."

"Advice! Oh is that all, well why didn't you say so. Advice eh? What kind of advice?" She asked.

"Well I need to find the Mouseketeers and since my father told me you've chased just about every cat in the area, I wondered if you could point me in the right direction please?" Willow asked politely.

"Har, har, so you want to chase them for yourself eh?" Meg began, and not waiting for a reply she continued. "Well I should wander down this road and keep going until you come to an ancient oak. You can't miss it because it's all twisty and on the edge of the path. Now, when you find it, bark up to the Brown Owl. He has a good vantage point up there and he'll point you in the right direction. I must say though, I wish you better luck than I had chasing them. They just seemed to disappear on me!" Meg mused doing her best to be helpful. Trouble was there weren't all that many dogs in the vicinity to talk to.

"Thank you for you help, Meg." Said Willow courteously but running off before she could start talking again, though he did promise to visit her soon. He meant it too. Willow was a nice dog.

It had occurred to Willow that the Brown Owl would still be asleep and that he might not like being woken but Willow didn't have time to waste. He'd have to risk it. Eventually he came upon the twisty ancient oak tree. Willow peered up into it. There amongst the twiggy 'witches broom' sprouting from the branches like the end of a besom, was Brown Owl sleeping peacefully. Now Willow didn't have a quiet way of making himself heard. He whined and whimpered but Owl did not hear him. He had to resort to a loud bark. Poor Brown Owl almost fell out of the tree.

"Hooo hoo, get those crows off me!" Owl hooted in his sleep.

"It's alright Owl, it's only Willow from Macracken Farm. I didn't mean to startle you Sir." Said Willow apologetically.

Owl ruffled his feathers and composed himself muttering about the unearthly hour and how he'd been rudely disturbed. Then he calmed down and gazed wonderingly at Willow.

"Please Sir could you point me in the right direction for the Mouseketeers?" Willow asked a little ashamed of himself for disturbing Owl.

"Mouseketeers, Mouseketeers! I most certainly can. I hope you chase them away. They hardly leave any mice for me. Pride themselves they really do with their trophies. Yes, yes by all means it's that way and when you come to a ramshackle cottage where no-body lives any more, well, that's where they hide out. How Barn Owl can stand living with that bunch I don't know." Owl said fluffing his feathers righteously.

As Willow thanked owl for his kindness, before he had even finished his sentence, owl dropped off to sleep again. Willow went on his way confident he would now be able to locate the Mouseketeers. Now he had a little skip in his step.

He came across the dark lane, owl had pointed to with his wing, quite quickly. At the bottom of it lay a ramshackle old cottage almost completely hidden with a wild growth of ivy. A perfect hide out for a wild bunch of cats. As Willow approached he could hear the Mouseketeers singing and dancing in some kind of wild party. They were chanting "One for you and three for me!" and falling about laughing raucously. Willow couldn't help but grin to himself. They sounded a lot of fun!

On his approach one of the cats heard him and shouted, "D.O.G. approaching!" whereby another cat shouted "Right men take your places!"

It was only a matter of seconds before Willow reached the garden at the back of the property and he was so sure he'd find the wild band of cats larking about. His ears had not deceived him. So where were they? He couldn't see them but he could sense them. How strange. Suddenly one of them spoke and Willow took it for granted that it must be the leader.

"Name! Rank!" Shouted Rascal the leader of the Mouseketeers.

Willow was a little taken aback. The voice had come from the old flower-bed that had been left to go wild.

"Er, Willow. Guard Dog of Macracken Farm." He replied undeterred.

"State your business Willow of Macracken Farm!" Rascal demanded.

"I should like to speak to the leader of the Mouseketeers on a matter of urgent business." Stated Willow firmly.

"Ah! Well that's different!" Declared Rascal "You see you're speaking to him!" He added and with that they all leaped forward from the undergrowth screaming,

"One for you and three for me!" With their claws at the ready and with sideways gins.

Well, no wonder Willow hadn't spotted them. Every one was a tabby cat and they were so well camouflaged against the earth, shrubs and woody vegetation, they were almost impossible to spot. Willow was impressed. The leader, Rascal, moved forward and bowed.

"Dear Sir, how may I be of assistance?" Rascal enquired swishing his tail.

Willow explained his special gift of dreaming about things that would become reality, premonitions in fact, and the Mouseketeers listened in awe. Then he told them about the latest one and how he needed their help to control a population boost of mice before it got out of control. At this the Mousketeers all said 'Hmmmm!' Then there was silence and Willow had to ask what Rascal thought about his plan.

"Well," began Rascal, "I'm sure we could deal with the task quite efficiently but how will you pay me?"

Willow didn't quite know what to say so he answered, "Well, Rascal, I don't have any money."

"No," Rascal said, "but what will you give me for my trouble, I really must have something, it's only fair." He mused.

"Well, what would you like?" Willow asked.

"Hmmmm. I think I would like a whole roast chicken all to myself without the others knowing." Rascal whispered in Willow's ear.

"Done." Willow said shaking paws with Rascal and with no idea how he was going to get hold of one of Susan's chickens, let alone roast it! He would worry about that later.

So Rascal and the Mouseketeers followed Willow back to Macracken Farm. What a sight that was! Luckily they were unobserved by humans. The Mouseketeers were always up for an adventure and besides, the wood mouse population in their own territory needed to recover though it wouldn't get out of hand with Barn Owl and Brown Owl to keep it in check.

On reaching Macracken farm, Willow had to introduce the Mouseketeers to his sheepdog family.

"One for you and three for me!" exclaimed the Mouseketeers in chorus.

"Sssshhhhh!" Said Willow "I don't want our owners to hear you!"

And so it was that the Mouseketeers lived on Macracken farm in secret having the time of their lives really, but pretending it was all hard work. They did a marvellous job in keeping down the numbers of rodents on the farm and by high summer, no plague of mice presented itself. Now all that was left was to obtain a roast chicken for Rascal. Oh dear.

Eventually Rascal sidled up to Willow asking about his chicken and hushing Willow because it was a private transaction between the two of them.

"Er yes, why is that?" Willow happened to ask.

"Well, actually I'm not that keen on mice. If you watch me next time we do our 'one for you and three for me' I toss one mouse out like I'm meant to for cats less privileged than myself, put one in my mouth so I don't starve and two go over my shoulder. The others don't know of course. They live on mice."

So now Willow knew! He promised Rascal he would get him a chicken somehow. He hadn't long to wait because the farmer and his wife had decided to hold sheepdog trials at their own farm. There was to be a big open-air feast afterwards for all their friends that came along. The television crew came and Willow recognised Robin Page, he liked him, his boots always smelled so interesting. All the animals were terribly excited especially when the food came out, although Oak and the other sheepdogs were far too busy being televised to take too much notice.

As luck would have it several roast chickens were put out and somebody began carving the cooked meat for the buffet. The minute Susan's helper sneezed, Willow leaped up, carefully grabbed one, without anyone seeing him, and bolted off to find Rascal who was waiting dribbling under a wheelbarrow.

"Fantastic!" meowed Rascal tucking in and nodding to Willow to pull a leg off for himself. Well they had become the best of friends and Susan's kitchen was saved from disaster thanks to Willow and the Mouseketeers. They deserved their chicken and had Susan known the facts she would have given Rascal ten chickens. Purrrfect!

THE END

The Adventures of Holly & Amber

The Hidden Valley & the Mystery of the Stolen Eggs

Holly the German shepherd stretched and yawned loudly. It had been a long holiday season, which had meant a lot of work for her master and mistress. Visitors had enjoyed a peaceful and secluded holiday at the picturesque 'Hidden Valley' caravan park near Ilfracombe. It was so beautiful here that even locals came to stay for a break away from their busy every day routines. Many people were attracted by the opportunities to go wildlife watching, in this secluded part of Devon. Holly had got to recognise one or two people that she particularly liked. They usually strolled along the Kingfisher or Buzzard Nature Trails making notes of natural history species. Holly could always tell because she would sniff their Wellington boots. She knew every scent along those trails. She knew when the fox came about, which flowers were blooming and which deer had come down to drink from the stream. She was an expert.

Early one morning mist swirled gracefully throughout the valley. Down by the small lake before people were about the water nymphs danced on the lily pads at the break of dawn. They did that every morning and were exquisitely beautiful to watch. Holly's favourite time was at sunset because her owners often let her have a last run about before bedtime with Amber her companion. Amber was also a German shepherd and rather over enthusiastic because she was young. She reminded Holly of herself years ago although Holly's patience often ran out because Amber wouldn't always listen to her natural history lessons. She hadn't yet learnt to concentrate and instead drifted off into fantastic daydreams. Never mind. Amber would soon be grown up and it was lovely to have a companion.

As the last visitor went off to bed, Holly's master and mistress prepared for the following day.

It was going to be busy again. Holly and Amber were let out for their run about so they chased each other to the lake. The sun set beautifully and the water nymphs were dancing again. Amber said she could hear old mother Moorhen bustling her black inky chicks off to bed. Holly said so could she and they listened intently enjoying the scents and sounds. The tiny sighs of damselflies and dragonflies could be heard all about as they settled amongst the vegetation for the night. The silvery bell-like voices of the tree nymphs, known as Dryads, echoed as they too settled in their trees. All was well. Amber and Holly loved the tranquillity of the lake. Holly told Amber the fish were called 'rudds' so Amber went dizzy watching them go round and round.

"Once we had carp in the lake too Amber, but an Otter came and ate the lot eventually. I don't think our master will restock the carp but our mistress said they were so pleased an otter was about, so it was alright even though it was annoying to loose all the fish." Holly was telling her.

Next morning was completely different. There was trouble. Apparently from the crack of dawn there had been quite a bit of activity. The water nymphs and dryads were looking quite perplexed and didn't know which way to turn. They had neither seen nor heard anything. Yet the wives of Blackbird, Robin and Blue Tit were all in tears. Someone had stolen their clutches of eggs! Well!

Lily the water nymph decided there and then to alert Holly the German shepherd. Perhaps she could use her nose and track down the culprit, with Amber's assistance.

"You never know what Holly may sniff out." Lily said to her brother Bud.

So Bud and Lily fluttered off to find Holly. They fluttered around the shop to check that the missing eggs weren't on sale by mistake, though of course they were not.

"No they're not in the shop and are too small for human consumption anyway." Bud said.

Unseen by humans, the two water nymphs located Holly and Amber. They whispered in their ears and the two dogs agreed to slip out somehow and see what they could scent. It was all such a mystery!

"Wonderful. We'll come back later to hear your report." Said Lily giving them each a hug for as magical as water nymphs were their sense of smell would never match Holly and Amber's.

Later Lily went off to find Squirrel but he swore he didn't take the eggs. It was true, he had an honest face and besides he couldn't have eaten *that* many eggs for breakfast. They weren't even hidden in his drey and Bud knew that for sure because he'd had a quick look when Lily was talking to Squirrel. No, squirrel was not the culprit here. They crossed him off their suspect list.

Next Bud went off to find crow, magpie and jay but they were all off site feeding elsewhere as it was such a fine day. They wouldn't use up food available close to home on a good day unless they were unwell. They usually left themselves a back-up. The crow family are smart birds and Bud checked all their nests and roosting areas for signs of broken egg shells, but as suspected, there were none. Again, as with squirrel, Lily and Bud crossed the crow family off their suspect list.

Meanwhile back in the private rooms of Hidden Valley, Amber was saying to Holly how they could make a dash for it out through the coffee shop.

"Oh no we can't." Holly was telling her firmly.

Amber looked surprised and a tad disappointed for she was raring to go, so Holly explained.

"For one thing we're not allowed to go where the food is, and for another our owners would be so disappointed in us for breaking rules they know Jolly well we know. No Amber, patience is a virtue. We must wait."

Amber sighed muttering how grown ups were so boring. She didn't complain though knowing that if she got Holly angry she'd be barked at and told off. Perhaps Holly was right after all since if an animal had taken the eggs, it would be the wrong time to search in any case. Holly said most wildlife came about at dawn and dusk times although there were exceptions like squirrels for example. "I must try to be patient," thought Amber.

Soon to their delight, someone came to let them out for a walk. Great! Now they could go about their task. Noses to the ground they both went about picking up scents though Amber let Holly go first, because she wanted to see her mentor in action. She stepped where Holly stepped, smelled what Holly smelled and slowly learned what made a good detective. How exciting. Maybe she would be as good one day. Holly was sure to teach her little protégé. They sped along the kingfisher trail, tails wagging.

"Sniff here Amber. Can you scent that musty smell?" Holly asked her.

"Oh yes I certainly can. What a pong!" Amber exclaimed.

"Well that's the scent of a fox, and see here…… those are its tracks." Holly explained.

The tracks led up into the wild wood and out of sight. They found nothing unusual along the Kingfisher trail, just the paw prints of their usual friends and a variety of wild flowers.

"Holly, why is this flower called a 'dog' violet?" Amber was nosing at some pretty deep blue-mauve flowers with glossy heart shaped leaves.

"Well, dog is used normally to describe a plant that either cures dog bites or doesn't smell, like dog rose, that's another example." Holly explained.

The weasel

"Well the dog down the road smells an awful lot!" Amber laughed.

"That's because his owner doesn't keep him clean dear." Chuckled Holly and on they went again.

Finding nothing unusual they moved on to the Buzzard Trail, a much longer walk. Here they found deer slots where the deer had crossed the route in order to get to the stream and drink. Stoat prints were also present in the wet mud but no smashed egg shells or other signs useful to their investigation.

"Stoat doesn't look like the culprit." Mused Holly and on they went again with noses to the ground.

Finally Holly pointed her nose at something moving in the undergrowth.

"What is it?" Amber whispered.

"Ssssh! Watch." Holly whispered back.

There, wrestling with something was a weasel. Holly could see that it didn't have a black tipped tail like that of a stoat's. The weasel was much smaller than a stoat too. They waited to see what it was doing. Sure enough, Weasel was dragging an egg down into a naturally formed stick pile at the edge of a traditional Devonshire hedge bank, to disappear down a small hole covered in moss where it lived. The weasel looked fraught and tired.

Holly would easily be able to find the weasel's den again, because it was marked by a huge holly tree with lots of lovely ferns and wildflowers growing all about. It wasn't certain that the weasel had taken all the other eggs of course but further investigation was most certainly necessary the two dogs decided.

"What do we do now?" Amber asked clearly delighted with their observation.

"We'll get back and report to Lily later when she calls for us." Holly decided.

After all, the two dogs were far too big to pursue Weasel down his hole. No, Lily and Bud would have to deal with it.

Holly and Amber took the scenic route back, crossing the little wooden bridge that took them over a chattering stream. She showed Amber where various bird's nests were and where the pink purslane grew. Amber was learning a lot and having a wonderful time. Holly really looked after her. The two dogs were warmly greeted when they arrived back. Holly was about ready for a rest now but Amber was going to chase her tail for a bit, until she fell over.

"I meant to do that so I can have a rest too." Amber fibbed.

Holly was amused but she was too polite to show it.

Lily and Bud arrived a little later so Holly was able to give them their report in full not missing a single detail. Lily was delighted but she sent Bud to talk to Weasel first. She'd go along a bit later to see all was going smoothly.

"He's a smooth talker and extremely tactful." She said grinning before making her way back to the lake.

Holly and Amber were anxious to know what had happened but they'd have to wait now. Bud would be a while dealing tactfully with Weasel. There would be a 'sorting out'. Weasel wasn't supposed to take so many eggs, not by Animal Law but then maybe he hadn't. A peaceful day passed by and finally a last night stroll was allowed for the two German Shepherds. No guessing where *they* went. Yes, straight to the lake.

The sun set golden as it slowly sank lower and lower on the horizon. The lake glistened gold and Lily was dancing on the lily pads as usual. Bud was counting the rudd because it relaxed him and helped him to sleep, better than counting sheep he reckoned. Holly and Amber waited for them patiently. The mallard duck had not yet settled for the night so Bud and Lily rode on their backs laughing and waited until the duck's took them leisurely to dry land, not that they couldn't fly themselves of course, but evenings were always playtime to water nymphs. And so they fluttered off the ducks to alight next to Holly and Amber grinning cheerfully.

"What happened?" Amber asked continuing, "Was Weasel the culprit?" She persisted.

"Oh yes, he was." Bud began. "I caught him with a stash of eggs, still warm in his den."

"Goodness, what did you do?" Holly wanted to know.

"Well after a chat with him, it turned out he had been starving as a youngster and has a bit of an obsession with hoarding food. He was actually wearing himself out working so hard collecting food he didn't need." Bud explained looking concerned.

"Poor dear." Holly sighed.

"Well, I had to explain that if he wanted eggs to eat, better not to take them all or there'd be no birds next year to lay any more. He hadn't thought of that. He obviously needs counselling so Lily is going to spend some time with him to help him put things back into perspective. He skipped too many lessons as a young weasel and therefore didn't get the education he should have had. I think he'll be fine, he just needs a friend to talk things out with." Bud explained earnestly.

"But best of all," began Lily "…all of the eggs were returned to their rightful parents as they hadn't gone cold. Isn't that wonderful? So there'll be plenty of baby birds for next year." Lily cried excitedly.

"Yes," Said Bud. "So, Mrs Blackbird, Mrs Robin and Mrs Blue Tit all have their unhatched chicks back. All is well once again thanks to the two of you." Bud patted their backs and made Holly and Amber feel nicely important.

"Yes, if it hadn't been for your wonderful detection work, we may have been too late to save the eggs. Perhaps we would never have caught Weasel at all. So thank you." Lily said gently hugging Holly and Amber in turn.

"Thank you, thank you, thank you!" chirped all the birds in unison.

And so it was that the mystery of the stolen eggs was solved and life at Hidden Valley resumed peacefully once again. It is only right that we too should congratulate the two German Shepherds. So, here we go, hooray for Holly and hooray for Amber! It just goes to show what an awful lot we humans could learn by listening to our animal companions more often.

THE END

Holly Saves Rainbow the Rabbit

Amber the German shepherd was busy with her Master, Martin, at The Hidden Valley Caravan Park. Meanwhile Martin's wife, Dawn, had taken Holly, another lovely German shepherd, to the new holiday park they now also owned. It was called Newberry and Holly liked the sound of it.

Dawn drove through a place called Combe Martin which was full of quaint little shops and lots of character. Holly watched from the window as children in the village slurped ice-creams in the hot sunshine. The car began to climb and wind slowly upwards affording her good views of the sea and rugged cliff faces.

Dawn turned the car off the road and drove into Newberry Farm and Holly was excited.
   "Come on Holly, out you jump. We've got lots to do you know." Dawn told her smiling and off they went to busy themselves with the day's events.

Rainbow was a little lop-eared grey rabbit with the saddest of expressions. Tommy had insisted mummy and daddy let him bring Rainbow on holiday to Newberry as they could-n't find anybody to look after the little rabbit when they were going to be away. Daddy didn't think it such a good idea but mummy gave in and finally daddy agreed. So now Rainbow was on holiday too. The family had spent a lovely week together, enjoying the village of Combe Martin with its coastal walks and general sea-side atmosphere. They'd come from the city and to be able to see the sea crashing on rocks and to hear buzzards mewing as they wheeled about the sky over the open fields was fantastic. Towards the end of their second and final week on holiday, a tragedy occurred.

Tommy was playing with Rainbow with the hutch door slightly open. Rainbow was nuzzling Tommy affectionately when all of a sudden Tommy sneezed and in that moment let go of the door. Rainbow bounced out happily doing little twisty leaps and dust bathing in a bare patch of ground. Tommy laughed and went to pick him up. All would have been well had it not been for a little Jack Russell belonging to the family in the adjacent caravan. The Jack Russell was a good little dog but loved to chase cats, rabbits, anything really just for the shear fun of it. The Jack Russell caught sight of Rainbow and gave chase. Rainbow's natural instincts told him to run. So Rainbow ran. Poor Tommy was helpless. All he could do was to shout out to his parents but they weren't quick enough to see what had happened leaving the poor child in a blubbering state of tears trying to explain.

For a long time the dog chased him relentlessly until two fields away Rainbow caught sight of a dark hole. He made for the hole, diving down to safety with the little dog barking outside. After a while the dog's owners whistled and like any good little dog, it returned obediently. It was just a hopeless mess of misfortune for poor old Rainbow.

Eventually when Rainbow had stopped shaking, he poked his little nose outside the burrow. The rest of him shortly followed. He found himself all alone in a large field that sloped down to views of the rugged coast and village life. Rainbow was lost. In his panic he hadn't noticed which way he'd run.
   "Tommy where are you!" snuffled poor Rainbow.

As the sun set other rabbits came out in the field to graze and chase about. They soon caught sight of Rainbow and teased him unkindly because he was different to them. Rainbow was grey, not brown like them and he had lop-ears.

"If you were a proper rabbit your ears would stick up when you listen and yours don't!" said Thistle, one of the wild rabbits unkindly.

The other rabbits were quite kind to Rainbow but kept at paws length. Rainbow knew he'd never fit in here and besides he was already missing his companion, Tommy.

Later on a fox came prowling about and all the wild rabbits went below ground. Rainbow had never seen a fox before and thought it was another kind of rabbit so he waited to make the fox's acquaintance.

The fox's mouth drooled when he saw Rainbow thinking him a tasty meal. The sly old fox crept closer and Rainbow began to feel uneasy. Luckily Rainbow was sat in front of one of the rabbit burrows. Rainbow suddenly felt something grip his tail and just as the old fox opened his jaws Rainbow was pulled to safety down the burrow.

"Whatever are you doing? You could have been eaten!" Buttercup exclaimed, a kindly old female wild rabbit.

"Oh I'm sorry I didn't know!" whimpered poor Rainbow.

Luckily Buttercup insisted that Rainbow stay the night in her burrow with her family where he would be safe so long as he kept out of the large buck rabbits way because he was fiercely territorial and wouldn't stand for intruders of any kind. So Buttercup hid Rainbow and at least he was dry and warm.

Meanwhile back at the caravans, Tommy's parents were telling Dawn all about their misfortune and how Tommy came to lose his darling rabbit.

"It's such a pity. We travel home tomorrow. Tommy is so upset." Tommy's mother was telling Dawn.

Holly the German Shepherd listened intently. Suddenly she had an idea.

"Woof!" Said Holly and out trotted the little Jack Russell that had chased Rainbow. He wanted to know which dog it was that had said 'Woof'.

Holly asked him which way he had chased Rainbow rabbit and the little dog was only too pleased to oblige.

"It was only a game Holly. I do hope everything will be alright. I didn't mean any harm you know," said the Jack Russell apologetically.

The wild rabbits

Holly understood and said she should be able to find Rainbow as long as he'd managed to spend the night safely somewhere.

Tommy's family were still talking to Dawn so Holly took the opportunity get a good sniff of Rainbow's hutch in an attempt to pick up Rainbow's scent. She then slipped away quietly. Holly soon covered the distance of two fields, only needing to leap one hedge. She then began snuffling about to hopefully trace either Rainbow Rabbit's or the Jack Russell scent that led to a burrow in the middle of a large open field. Just as well it hadn't rained or all the scent would have been washed away. Luckily this was Buttercup's burrow and Rainbow was still inside asleep.

"Rainbow, Rainbow, are you there?" Holly called softly.

Rainbow lifted his head to see Holly's muzzle poking down the burrow and panicked.

"Oh Mother Buttercup, Mother Buttercup, there's a big fox coming to get me!" Rainbow wailed.

Buttercup stamped her feet which told all the rabbits to remain safely in the burrow.

"That's odd. It doesn't smell much like a fox to me. Not a bit musty." Buttercup muttered.

Holly had to explain that she was not a fox at all, that she was a German Shepherd come to rescue Rainbow and take him home before it was too late.

"Your family go home tomorrow Rainbow so if you want to see Tommy again you must trust me to take you back." Holly said urgently.

"Do you want to go home?" Buttercup asked kindly.

"Oh yes, yes I do!" Rainbow whimpered.

Buttercup nuzzled Rainbow goodbye and slowly nudged him out of the burrow. Rainbow gasped as Holly's jaws came down on him. He shut his eyes as Holly picked him up by the scruff of his neck and away they went over the fields, over the hedge, and back to the caravans to find Tommy. After a while Rainbow wasn't afraid any more and actually enjoyed the ride.

"Weeeeeeeeeeeee!" He called out laughing. Thistle rabbit poked his head out of his warren to see Rainbow having fun with what he thought was the biggest fox he'd ever seen. Thistle gasped and wished he'd got *cool* friends like that. Then he thought shamefully that maybe he would have done if he'd been more pleasant to Rainbow. Too late now for the gallant Rainbow Knight was obviously off on another adventure and leaving the rabbit field forever.

Thistle was sorry and was never rude again.

Dawn was now calling for Holly. Holly could hear her but she couldn't bark a reply with Rainbow rabbit in her mouth. She returned as quickly as possible to gasps of delight and much praise. Tommy was delighted of course and Rainbow nuzzled him happily.

"You're the most beautiful rabbit in the entire world and I'm so glad you've come home." Tommy whispered to Rainbow.

Now Rainbow felt much better. All the jibes he took from the wild rabbits meant nothing now. Rainbow fluffed himself up feeling nicely important. It is often surprising how just a few simple kind words can make the world of difference to somebody.

When the excitement had calmed down and Rainbow was safely back in his hutch Tommy was telling Dawn all about their garden at home where Rainbow could race around and play in safety.

"All rabbits should be able to run about sometimes and not be in a hutch all day long. I shouldn't like being shut in all day everyday if I were a bunny." Tommy said.

"Oh yes…." smiled his mother "…. The garden's all fenced in and quite safe. Daddy put chicken wire at the bottom of the fence and buried it 3ft down beneath the soil so the rabbit wouldn't dig its way out. Tommy and Rainbow often play together for hours after school, though I did warn Tommy not to let Rainbow out whilst we were on holiday didn't I darling?"

"Yes Mummy," replied Tommy looking at his feet and twiddling his thumbs.

"Never mind, these things happen and it's all better now thanks to Holly," laughed Dawn.

Little did Holly know that before Tommy's family went home, they would leave a present just for her in reception to thank her for being such a good and kind dog. 'Amber would never believe this story……' thought Holly to herself as Dawn drove her back to Hidden Valley Caravan Park to get Martin's lunch.

THE END

Woodland Adventures

Tutshill Wood & the Wicked Witch

Blackberry, Bundle and Bramble rabbits were playing nicely together on the edge of Shearford Lane by a big beech tree, where they lived. Shearford Lane is an ancient packhorse route but people today walk down it enjoying a country walk to the end of the lane, then across the bridge and perhaps wander through Tutshill Wood.

Now on this occasion it was quite late in the day and not a soul was about so the wildlife had come out to hunt for dinner or merely to play. Blackberry, Bundle and Bramble were having a wonderful time playing hide and seek but their mother called out not to go too far in case they were to become lost. Luckily the young rabbits were well behaved and always did as they were told.

"Well I'm going to the stream now to get a drink. Back in a minute," announced Bundle still giggling because Bramble was still trying to tug her on the tail.

It was a glorious evening and Bramble and Blackberry could hear their mother singing merrily from their nearby warren. Now Bundle was a long time in returning from his drink down by the stream. Bramble and Blackberry didn't want to alarm their mother so they went off to look for him.

Skipping down Shearford Lane was a lot of fun. They dashed in and out of the vegetation and came to a tumble down stone bridge no longer used by people. Opposite the bridge spring water flowed at ground level and this was where rabbits and other creatures could safely drink. Ideal if you are but a small animal. No chance of being swept away by the current. The River Yeo flowed a little further down. But alas, call as they might Bundle was not to be found!

A breeze fluttered a spider's web and the leaves rustled as if chattering.
   "Do you think the leaves are trying to tell us something?" Bramble asked his brother.
   "Not sure. Could be," whispered Blackberry.

They both had a sinking feeling. They feared for their missing sister.

At that moment they both heard silvery tinkling bells. The sound was pretty but it tickled their ears.

All was well for it was only the Dew Fairy appearing before them. She was very beautiful. She had little crystal dew-drop gems on her garments that shone every colour as the evening sun touched them. Her dress was silvery-blue and free flowing

"Aren't you supposed to be with your mother?" asked the Dew Fairy.

"Er, yes ma'am but you see we've come to look for our missing sister. She only came down here for a quick drink," Bramble explained.

"Well now, I'll see what I can do but remember one thing…" she told them earnestly and looking at them both to make sure they were listening before continuing.

"…. don't talk to any strangers. Don't forget now," she said vanishing as quickly as she had appeared.

So Blackberry and Bramble wandered farther down the lane, crossing the wooden bridge and out into a huge open field where their mother often took them for chasing games. There was no sign of Bundle. Next they crossed the field and headed towards an ancient oak tree that marked the entrance to Tutshill Wood. Perhaps Bundle was hiding there. She did so love hide and seek.

"Bundle is very naughty running off and putting us to all this worry." Blackberry complained.

"It's so unlike her." Bramble mused.

Eventually they reached the ancient oak tree but Bundle was not there. Bramble thought he heard something but he couldn't make out what exactly. He strained his ears. No just a tree branch squeaking perhaps. So Bramble and Blackberry hopped along into Tutshill Wood passing the weir and listening to a green woodpecker's yaffle call.

'We'd better hurry up. Green Woodpecker says it might rain,' they both thought to themselves. They often thought the same things.

The rabbits scampered this way and that looking for Bundle and in truth got a little bit lost. An old woman wearing a long black dress was busily collecting herbs, or at least they thought they were herbs. Actually it was poison ivy and only as the two rabbits ventured closer did they discover this. Now Bramble well recalled the Dew Fairy's warning but Blackberry in desperation to find Bundle had started to speak and to ask which way to go. Bramble dug him in the ribs too late.

"Which way or witch way!" cackled the ugly old crone.

Both rabbits were terrified.

"I'll take it you mean witch way. Want to go my way do you?" She said, her evil eyes flashing.

Now they both realised she was an evil old witch and were probably in a lot of trouble.

They were right for as she raised her finger a flash of yellow struck them both on the chest. There was a big puff of smoke and Bramble and Blackberry suddenly found that they were now tiny! The old witch cackled and wandered off deeper into the wood, her footsteps thundering. The two little rabbits clung to each other but suddenly the wind picked up.

"Quick brother grab on to this leaf!" Yelled Bramble as the howling wind deafened their tiny voices.

The rabbits clung on to a bronze coloured beech leaf as the gusts of wind became stronger and stronger. Suddenly they were flying through the air as if on a magic carpet. All the other autumnal leaves swirled about them and headed for the weir only to be washed away to…. where? They didn't know. Luckily their leaf sailed clear of the weir but it still alighted in the middle of the River Yeo and the current was strong. The leafy boat went round and round and they were lucky not to have capsized. Bramble and Blackberry's tiny screams were lost to all but the water boatmen further down the river where the water became still and trout sometimes gathered.

The leaf came to rest a while in the stillness of the pool though the river still flowed and it would be but a matter of minutes before they'd be sailing on down the river again. Bramble saw a tail swish beneath the surface of the water and a dread filled his whole body. Luckily the water skaters and a water boatman came to the rescue and pulled their leaf safely to shore, gesturing to the rabbits to keep very still and quiet lest they alert the dozing trout of their presence, for they were now bite size.

How good it was to feel dry soil beneath their feet. Bramble and Blackberry couldn't thank the water skaters and water boatman enough.

"It's a curious thing. We've never seen your kind before, well not so small, but you're the second rescue we've done today!" exclaimed the water boatman.

Bramble and Blackberry's hearts lifted.

"Oh have you found our sister. Is she alive and well? Oh do please tell us Sir," cried Bramble excitedly as Blackberry nodded enthusiastically.

"Why yes, yes indeed. She got rather wet falling off her leaf and it was a near thing old fish face asleep down there didn't swallow her up," laughed the water boatman.

Tutshill Wood

"Where is she?" Blackberry pleaded.

"Ah now, let me see. Ah yes, she went in with Mrs Woodmouse down by the white clover clump," pointed the water boatman with his spidery black leg.

They thanked their new friends very much for their kindness and off they went in search of Mrs Woodmouse.

Luckily Mrs Woodmouse was inside her mouse hole dwelling and received them gladly.

"Come in my dears and get warm." She told them.

Both rabbits were feeling in a state of shock after their terrible ordeal and were glad to be welcomed into Mrs Woodmouse's cosy home. In the corner of the little parlour was Bundle. She was wrapped up in a grass woven blanket and was dozing in between sneezes.

"Oh Bundle! We thought we'd never see you again!" cried her brothers as they swiftly hopped over to hug her.

"Oh my darling brothers, I thought I was lost forever." She exclaimed.

Mrs Woodmouse brought out a tea tray of toasted grass-seed cake and the little rabbits ate heartily exchanging similar stories of encountering the wicked witch and being swept away by the wind. Bundle hadn't been able to hold on to her leaf and had almost drowned but she was feeling much better now. Mrs Woodmouse had listened in awe to their tales and said she'd certainly make sure none of her children ventured into Tutshill Wood.

Blackberry decided they had better get home to see if they could find the Dew Fairy. Maybe she could break this awful spell.

"Besides Mother will be sick with worry!" exclaimed Blackberry.

They thanked Mrs Woodmouse for her kindness and ventured off together staying very close to each other. It was dangerous to be so tiny. Even the woodmice were considerably bigger than they were. Being so tiny meant that their walk home would be a mammoth task. The rabbits seemed to walk for mile upon mile, poor things. The sun went down and as the moon slowly rose they decided they could walk no further. They huddled together and slept. At least they were together now, that was some comfort.

Little did they realise that they were in fact sleeping in the middle of an ancient fairy ring. Here they were protected. It was also here that the Dew Fairy found them safe and well, albeit tiny! She sat by their sides and watched over them thankful that they were unhurt from their ordeal. Bramble awoke to find the Dew Fairy sitting with them and while his brother and sister slept he related his story to her. She shook her head making tut-tutting sounds as she listened.

"Can't you break this spell?" He asked her.

"Alas I can not! The only way to break such a powerful curse is to find the witch that gave it to you, recover the spell and use it on her." The Dew Fairy explained.

"But it will take me days to get back to Tutshill Wood the size I am!" Bramble wailed.

The Dew Fairy said she would enchant a leaf for him to travel on. All he had to do was sit on it and 'think' where he wanted to go and the leaf would take him. When he was ready to return he merely had to whistle or thump his feet and it would be there.

"Now you know what you have to do Bramble. I'll sit with your brother and sister. You must break this spell yourself dear one."

With a parting hug, Bramble leapt onto his magic leaf and was away.

Travelling on a magic leaf was a lot more fun than Bramble had anticipated. His tiredness now completely gone he was ready to defeat the evil old witch. Soon Bramble was guiding the leaf into Tutshill Wood, deeper and deeper he went. The moon was bright and full and he could see well in the moonlight.

He caught sight of a fire flickering in the distance. He had located the ugly witch stirring a deadly potion in a cauldron over the safely contained fire. He flew towards her. 'Gosh' he thought she was even uglier than he remembered, almost too ugly to look at in fact. She had warts and wrinkles, a huge aquiline nose and a pointy chin. Her beady eyes soon caught sight of him and they flashed in anger at him. He alighted to the ground and turned his leaf over to hide himself from being struck by another spell. The old witch stamped and stamped on all the leaves. She almost got him but he moved just in time. He let out a scream and a last groan pretending she'd got him and oh how that evil old witch laughed until her sides hurt. She was so busy revelling in her success that Bramble was able to zoom up in his leaf and slip into her smelly old pocket. There he stayed patiently waiting.

The hours went by and eventually she went back to her underground cavern, returning the cauldron to the kitchen stove and getting out jars in which to pour her deadly poison she'd been brewing in the moonlight. The old witch had to refer to her spell book several times and Bramble hopped from her pocket onto the large wooden table when she had gone to bed. Bramble had been spotted, by the witch's warty toad friend, who was squatting in the corner of the cavern, but he made no signs to alert his mistress, strange. He didn't even croak.

So Bramble went about the business of finding the spell in the large book. The pages were heavy to turn but he managed somehow. Eventually after an hour or more he found the spell he wanted. He thumped his feet for his magic leaf. The leaf arrived and on he hopped. He'd have to lure the old witch into the kitchen, as the sun would shine through a little opening in the cavern and he needed her to be in the rays of the sun when he cast the spell. All three rabbits had been struck by the same spell in sunlight hours so therefore he must be patient and await the sun.

The toad stared at Bramble as he zoomed around the kitchen on his magic leaf. He almost seemed friendly somehow. Finally he moved towards the sleeping witch and landed on her nose to wake her up. She was a light sleeper and soon leapt to her feet. She was still half asleep as she tried to chase Bramble but the minute she was in the kitchen and the rays of sun alighted on her shoulders Bramble cast the spell. Her face was one of shear terror for she hadn't given Bramble any credit as to be intelligent enough to give her some of her own medicine. In a puff of smoke she was suddenly tiny and running about with her hands to her head. Then she stopped and made to climb up the table leg to try and reach her spell book.
"I'll get you yet!" She screamed.
Poor Bramble was still tiny. It hadn't worked. What was he to do now? Suddenly the warty toad was hopping after his mistress.
'Time to get out of here,' thought Bramble but just as he was about to jump back on the magic leaf, the toad stuck out his big sticky tongue and ate the witch!

Suddenly there was a sound of tinkling bells and a flash of rainbow colours. Puff! Bramble was his original size again. He looked across for the toad but stars danced all about him and crystal lights flashed every colour. He too was changing in form. There, crouching on the floor was a beautiful Fairy Prince. His silvery wings glistened and he stood up and smiled kindly at Bramble.
"You saved me! You have broken the spell of a thousand years! How may I repay you?" Said the Prince in a quiet voice and choking back tears of relief.
"I want nothing Sir, only to be back in the field with the Dew Fairy. I need to see if my brother and sister have returned to their proper size." Bramble sighed.
"That can be arranged." smiled the Prince who whistled at the now tiny magic leaf, casting star dust over it from his pocket.
In a puff of smoke the leaf was big enough to carry them both. Soon they were in the field

with the Dew Fairy and the now properly sized Blackberry and Bundle. Thank goodness the spell had worked. All was well and the wicked old witch was no more.

The rabbits skipped merrily home.

"Wait until we tell mother all about our adventures!" Cried Bramble happily and they bid the Dew Fairy and the Fairy Prince goodbye.

The Dew fairy was so surprised to see the Fairy Prince she hardly knew what to say.

"I heard about the legend years ago but I never dreamed it was true!" She said.

He laughed and they sailed away on the magic leaf together never to be lonely again.

THE END

Anchor Wood & the Mysterious Monk

When Spinney the squirrel was born, her eyes were never as good as those of her brother and sister. Spinney didn't see anything sharply but she managed to get by, although she was slower than her siblings owing to the fact she needed to be more careful when leaping through the trees. Other squirrels rushed on by leaving Spinney to clumsily make her way as best she could. The other animals of Anchor Wood noticed her slowness but were too kind to comment in case they upset dear Spinney whom they loved as a friend. She was a good-hearted squirrel and would do anything for anybody if she could.

One day as Spinney went about her way, a good fairy appeared before her.

"No-one but I have noticed your troubles dear Spinney," said the fairy kindly.

Spinney smiled at the fairy knowing that others *had* noticed but had dared not say.

"What am I to do about it then if you please?" asked Spinney hopefully.

"Well Spinney…" began the fairy continuing, "we believe your partial blindness is a contact blindness which happened when the farmer sprayed his crops. Your mother moved her nest here to Anchor Woods where she knew you and your siblings would be safe. The farm here, below the wood, has livestock not crops, so no sprays are used. Unfortunately you were the last to be moved and I believe you were exposed to the chemical spray that the wind swept over you. I've talked among my own people in our World of Faerie, and it is believed that if you wash your eyes in the water of The Dripping Well every day, you may regain your full eyesight," said the fairy.

"Oh that's wonderful. Is the water of The Dripping Well magical then?" asked Spinney happily.

Anchor Wood

"The water runs through under ground caverns and through many mineral rocks before dripping out as it does, from the face of the 'well'. Not a well at all in the real sense, but the formulae within the water is powerful enough to be beneficial to the eyes. My people use the water often but it is not for drinking. Drink from the spring further up the wood for there are many in Anchor Woods to choose from. Bathe the eyes with the water from the Dripping Well and you will be surprised at what you may see…. Perhaps it is magical Spinney." Said the fairy as she faded away back onto the ether, a place beyond this world.

Spinney was overjoyed! She bathed her eyes every day and slowly, very slowly her eyesight seemed to improve. Three full moons came and went and her eyesight was as good as her brothers or sisters or any squirrels for that matter. What a joy to be able to see clearly. Now Spinney could keep up with the other animals and nobody seemed to notice her cumbersome movements because she wasn't slow and didn't need to be so careful anymore. What fun to leap through the trees and just *be*.

As time went on, summer approached along with the children's school holidays. Children often came down into the woods to play games or walk through the woodland to reach the Tarka Trail. Now, there were two extremely naughty children who always dropped litter. They knew they weren't supposed to but they did it anyway much to the animals despair, for the woodland was their home and the children and other people were merely visitors. That's how the creatures of Anchor Woods saw it anyway.

Mark brought his friends down into the woods one night to drink fizzy pop. He discarded the empty cans down through the trees and also into the pond by the Dipping Well. Poor old Water-Rail, a shy bird with red legs and pretty grey-blue and brown plumage, was unfortunate to cut his foot on the sharp tin can for he couldn't see it buried beneath the green duckweed. He shrieked in pain but luckily his wound was not too deep. He healed swiftly but never returned again.

The cans in the woods rolled to the bottom of the steep incline. They contained residue beer, which was sweet to smell. Almost a whole population of violet ground beetles were attracted to it and drowned in the left over beer, for once inside they could not get out. The fairies and dryads were getting angry! Even wood mice and shrews got trapped inside drink bottles and died.

The following day Mark's brother Josh smashed a glass bottle, by throwing it away in the undergrowth. Another bottle was thrown on top of the first and they both smashed into nasty shards of glass that protruded from the vegetation. A dog lay down here to await his owner, he was playing a game, the same game he played every morning. The poor dog cut himself terribly and his owner, much distressed, rushed him to the vets for stitches. Not so lucky was Old Red the fox. He cut his paw terribly. No vet for him. Old Red is a wild animal, and they have to take care of themselves. Luckily the good fairy was at hand. She nursed him back to health.

Mostly the children were very good and never dropped litter but the two boys were not good at all. They were brothers and encouraged each other to be naughty. As time went on the vexation of the animals and magical creatures of the wood drew to a climax. Spinney wondered what was going to happen for something surely would!

That evening down by the Dripping Well Spinney bathed her eyes using a hartstongue fern pushed into the face of the Dripping Well. The water ran off the leaf and this helped to guide the water onto her paws and then onto her face. She watched the water dipping off this beautiful fern surrounded by green crinkle edged liverwort that covered the face of this lovely Dripping Well. Spinney felt refreshed. She sighed and heard the words of the good fairy again…

"You will be surprised at what you may see." echoed her silvery voice in Spinney's head.

Looking up Spinney saw a grey monk. She could not see his face but he was wearing a grey cloak, belted with twine and his hood covered his identity. He hovered above the ground and Spinney realised that the monk was a ghost, but even so she was not afraid. The monk meant her no harm. She knew the Dripping Well was on an alignment with Tawstock Church and that humans had lost much of the ancient history of the place. Even the Dripping Well only had its commemorative surround built in 1865 yet, the Dripping Well was considerably older. It was a mysterious place but Spinney loved it.

Spinney watched the monk hovering there. He moaned a little before he spoke.

"Ooooooooh, I am vexed, oooooooooh I am vexed!" He said in a restless sort of way.

Spinney bit her lip. Should she say something?

"OOOOOOH I AM VEXED!" shouted the monk, his voice now booming through the woodland.

Other animals were alert now and came to sit beside Spinney.

"Cool, a ghost!" Said her brother

"Sssssshh!" said all the other animals.

The monk then spoke to them all.

"I am angry at the disrespect of humans. This is indeed an ancient woodland, that *has* been coppiced in *modern* times, but that doesn't make it a modern woodland. Ah I have seen it all, all the history. I am the woodland's protector. The woodland is not respected. I will curse those that harm the woodlands. So be it! The sinners that fall will only succeed in breaking my curse by repenting with good actions. I am relentless and *angry*. *Feeeel* my wrath. *Oooooooooh* I am vexed!" wailed the monk gruffly before vanishing.

Well! The animals gasped in astonishment. Whatever would happen? Yet at the same time they were delighted that Anchor Woods had a protector. What would happen on Friday night when those two naughty boys came to throw their rubbish about! Oh my! The anticipation was almost too much but Friday night came about soon enough and the animals kept well out of sight. This time Mark had not brought his friends, only his naughty brother.

"Come on Josh, hurry up. There's no-one about. Let's have a can of beer then."

"Mark, you know we're not supposed to, we're not old enough and Mum will go *ballistic* if she finds out."

"Ah don't worry, she'll never know," went the conversation.

Mark looked much older than he really was and had bought some beer from the local shop. After both boys had drunk from the cans, Josh decided he didn't like the taste of beer anyway and threw the can and its contents into the woods. Mark finished his drink and did the same. Each time a can hit the woodland floor a golden flash seemed to spark from them. Unnerved the boys made their way home swiftly. It was getting dark now and they were already late.

They had to walk to the other side of town. It was a couple of miles or so but when Mark put his key in the door a bright golden flash enveloped them both and they found themselves back in the woods again! The boys were astonished. They were face to face with their beer cans lying in the leaf litter. Stubbornly Mark made off for home again but Josh had a guilty pang.

"Maybe the woods are telling us we have to pick up the cans, brother?" He suggested.

"Nah! Must have fallen asleep or something," replied Mark rather red in the face.

"Well I haven't been dreaming, neither have you and that was a long walk."

It was no use. Mark made his brother walk home a second time and just as he put the key in the latch again, another flash of golden light found them back in the woods yet again!

Now they were both panicking. Josh and Mark began to argue. It was extremely late and no doubt they would both be in trouble when they got home. Unknown to both boys, their father new where they went on Friday nights and he was coming after them, concerned there'd been an accident. When their father appeared in the woods it was momentary relief on both parts but then the boys blurted out their story and their father became angry. For one thing he didn't believe such a silly story and for another it was pretty obvious that Mark had been drinking beer, for it was on his breath.

"Pick up those cans! I'll not have sons of mine being litter-louts. What kind of an example is this to your brother eh Mark!" shouted their father.

Well, that was the start of it. Both boys were grounded for two weeks and the shop was informed that Mark was not the age he pretended to be so he could never buy beer again. Little did the family know that had their father not ordered them to retrieve the discarded beer cans, the spell would never have been broken......

So, with lessons well learned, Anchor Woods was at peace again and the creatures that lived there were safe.

THE END

Moorland Adventures

The Adventures of Riff & the Magic Lantern

Not many boys and girls know but, in the dog world there are kings, queens, princes and princesses, just as there are today in human society. Such royal blood in a dog is rare indeed, yet deep in the heart of Dartmoor, a young she-dog named Riff reigned over all the other dogs in the land. She had descended from a long line of queens. When Riff came to live with her new Master and Mistress, the fairies had been instructed by Earth Mother herself, to carry a special present to Riff in order to protect the new Queen and her Queendom.

Riff's gift was a magic lantern. The lantern lit up blue-silver every night all by itself. The lantern gathered the energy of the sun by day and shone it out at night. It was very pretty and hung on an ancient tree in Riff's courtyard. She guarded it proudly. Riff's Master and Mistress merely thought this enchanted lantern was a Moth trap since many species of moth danced in the pretty light. Riff's owners loved all wildlife, and were enchanted by its mystical light, even though they were unaware of its magical powers.

That night a full moon cast its beautiful silvery beams of light upon the mysterious land of Dartmoor. Riff sighed contentedly and gazed up at the twinkling stars flashing silver and gold above a frost bitten land. Riff gazed at her lantern and saw that it blinked calmly the blue-silver light signalling that all was well in her Queendom. When the moon was at its highest a deep undulating bark waxed and waned as the wind blew the sound to and fro. Riff listened…

"Ralph, Ralph Ralph!"

Yes she knew that bark it was an Old English sheepdog called Ralph. He was her first knight and protector of her realm. Next there sounded a shorter sharper bark of "Woof, Woof, Woof!" This was Woof, a good old friend to Riff. He was a collie-cross with a high intellect to match Ralph's and Riff's and thus he was second knight and protector of the Realm. Finally a tawny owl hooted in the distance to be answered by a second closer to home and a wily old fox barked once. Queen Riff, seated beneath her magic lantern, barked three times in acknowledgement to them all and to bid them all good night. It was the same routine every night, a good way of communicating that all was well on the various farms on Dartmoor and on the surrounding moorland and countryside. Riff had eyes everywhere and

Queen Riff & her Magic Lantern

that was important because a Queen has to know all there is to know all of the time in order to sort out any problems that might occur. Thus, Riff was a very good Queen and all the wild creatures that lived in Riff's Queendom felt safe and cared for. If at any time a creature was in trouble or a human friend belonging to that creature, all that had to be done was to sing out and Riff would hear. Help would always follow one way or another.

Come morning a similar routine would occur of barking dogs, singing blackbirds and calling pheasants. All sounds of the countryside and loved as such by all real country lovers.

New Year's Eve saw many human festivities including loud fireworks that frightened pets and wildlife, for the aftershock of such explosions was felt deeply by them all. A new family had moved to Dartmoor. A lovely family with bright young children and a shining Black Labrador were among those celebrating. Unfortunately as soon as the fireworks began the poor dog was so terrified she chewed through her lead and bolted over the hedge to lose herself on the unfamiliar moorland. At every bang, and there were many, the dog ran further and further from home whimpering and whining her distress. It was dark and the mist was sweeping in until she couldn't see one paw in front of the other! Finally the poor dog huddled shivering beneath a gnarled, windswept hawthorn tree, covered her face with her paws and when all the noise had stopped she realised just how lost she had become. "Master!" she barked but no-one could hear her now, no-one but an old wily fox and even he was hidden by the mist. She tried to follow his bark but the wind played tricks and blew all sound hither and thither. It was useless.

Meanwhile, Riff's magic lantern was flashing away furiously signalling trouble. Since Ralph was only ever tethered to his kennel, he was able to slip his collar and come to Riff's assistance. She could not go herself as Queen, because it just wasn't protocol and until she had puppies of her own there would be no-one to take on the role of Queen if anything happened to Riff, so her Knights always fought on her behalf. Ralph arrived, bowing his head courteously. Riff had the magic lantern in her mouth by its circular handle. She pawed it over to Ralph who in turn took it in his mouth.

"Now, all you have to do is follow the bright light. If the light becomes dull, then you are going in the wrong direction so turn about until it becomes strong again. It will bring you home safely too. Good luck dear Ralph, first knight and protector of my realm." Riff said and Ralph nodded, turned about and vanished in seconds into the mist as he dashed across the moorland. Luckily the enchanted light of the magic lantern penetrated through the mist with ease.

Ralph seemed to follow the light for quite some time. He had never used the magic lantern before and hoped it wouldn't let him down. He crossed a stream, leaped a hedge, followed an old stone wall for a while and passed many ancient stones even he didn't recognise. Ralph had always lived on the moorland. His mistress was a horse-rider and he would often follow her on her jaunts. A lovely life he had and he was so patient with the children too. Emily was always falling off her pony when her mother first taught her to ride and it was Ralph who would be there to lick her wounds so that tears soon turned to laughter. What would Emily say now if she could see her darling dog charging across the moorland in the pitch dark on an errand for the Queen and bearing a magic lantern?

Eventually Ralph came upon a wind-swept hawthorn tree. At first he thought there was a black shadow beneath the tree until that black shadow whimpered and whined. The light from the lantern flashed silver and Ralph knew he had found his quarry.

"Come along with me young whippersnapper and I will take you to safety." Ralph Barked gallantly.

The black Labrador smiled gratefully, she couldn't bark through her snuffles but followed quietly along as Ralph soothed her with fairy tales and other stories. The black Labrador was called Jet. Jet was shy but was comforted by the pretty light of the lantern and Ralph's fatherly way.

It had been a long night for Ralph and his mission wasn't over until he had made contact with Queen Riff to return the precious lantern. Ralph's paws ached and Jet felt cold and tired from her ordeal. When they arrived in the Queen's courtyard Riff was waiting for them anxiously. Ralph said that all was well and Jet explained how frightened she had been with all the explosions. She wasn't even sure if her human family were alive any more. Then Riff had to explain about fireworks and that humans used them to celebrate certain events. This was beyond Jet's understanding because she said, if she made a lot of noise by barking too much, she would be told off by her owners. Oh dear! Well any dog will know that that is true of most owners.

With the magic lantern returned, Ralph said he'd take Jet back to his kennel where she could sleep. He'd leave his owners to return Jet in the morning as she didn't live far away by road and everybody knew everybody in their vicinity so no problems. By the time Ralph arrived home there was a bit of a commotion at the farmhouse as some people had lost their dog which had been frightened by the fireworks. They were asking all the villagers to please keep their eyes open.

"Quick, follow me!" Said Ralph and Jet followed him to his kennel. He had to slip on his collar before his owner saw that he was free. Jet went inside the kennel and sat down and Ralph sat outside barking. Shortly the farmer appeared to discover Jet, the missing dog everyone was so worried about. Ralph was rewarded and Jet was reunited with her owners quicker than expected. Jet was deeply grateful to Ralph, Queen Riff and the magic lantern. All was well and at peace on Dartmoor once again….. for a while that is.

One night beneath the protection of the holly tree in the courtyard, a secret meeting of Queen Riff and her two knights took place. They were discussing matters of farmland, moorland and surrounding countryside and the creatures that lived there. They talked so long that soon dawn was breaking and some of the day birds began to sing. A grumpy old magpie came about, took a fancy to the pretty blue lantern and stole it! Needless to say there was up roar. Since dog's cant fly no-one was able to follow the magpie and this left Ralph and Woof having to undertake many life-threatening missions without the protection of the magic lantern. The fairies who had given the magic lantern to Queen Riff were furious and ready to punish the culprit.

Weeks went by with no sign of the lantern. Eventually a flock of pigeons located the lantern but it was too heavy for them to retrieve. It was decided to contact the tawny owl, a dangerous business for owl had powerful talons. Most of the pigeons hid themselves in positions where they could watch the lantern, in case magpie decided to move it again whilst the bravest pigeon puffed himself up and flew off in search of the tawny owl.

The poor pigeon was very frightened of the tawny owl and her big talons. For some time pigeon couldn't make himself heard, fear rendering him speechless. Eventually he managed to ask the tawny owl, in the nicest possible way, to retrieve the magic lantern for Queen Riff. Little did the pigeon know that the owl was one of Queen Riff's spies so he needn't have been afraid after all. Tawny owl was so pleased and even though it was still daylight and the owl should still have been asleep she alighted from her snug roosting branch to follow pigeon to magpie's nest. Once there, tawny owl snatched away the magic lantern from magpie and returned it safely to Queen Riff who cried for joy at its return. Riff gave her new friends the pigeons the status of Guardian's of the Realm and they were deeply honoured. As for magpie, owl delivered him to the fairies. The fairies were so outraged with the magpie that they turned him into a humble Jenny Wren so that he might lose his greedy ways and learn a jolly good lesson.

THE END

Hannah Encounters Exmoor

Hannah hadn't had an easy upbringing. Now in her early teens she found herself living with a new family and starting again. Today would be the first time her supportive Godmother would attend an Exmoor wildlife walk, bringing her family in tow to meet Hannah's new guardian. It was important that everything went well because Hannah was extremely happy now and she wanted the news to go back positively to her old family.

The day began well. The weather was calm, a little rain pending, nothing much. The party met during the afternoon, at Breakneck Hole, where they parked their cars. It was a short distance from the Black Venus Inn on Exmoor. All had binoculars at the ready and were attired with boots, coats, hats, thumb sticks etc in readiness for the rugged terrain ahead. The party walked along the road for someway and then veered left through a gateway and up over the moorland passing the Bill Hill stone and others along the way. There were several menhirs and archaeological artefacts on route. It was certainly a very special place thought Hannah.

Hannah was nervous but quite keen to show off what she'd learnt about the countryside under the care of her new friend. A stonechat called from the top of a gorse bush. It was a male with a striking black head and eye stripe. Hannah pointed him out and also the female with her softer colours watching from nearby. Milkwort grew here, a pretty delicate blue flower that Hannah identified for her cousin. Lousewort, sphagnum moss and sundew were just some of the plants special to Exmoor and Hannah's new guardian had shown her exactly where to find them all. Once he'd even shown her a pair of merlins, Britain's smallest bird of prey and quite rare but alas they were not about today. In fact even the mewing buzzard did not reveal itself.

The windswept hawthorn trees grew in such strange shapes along the hedgerows, their twisted forms like ghostly waifs in places. It was raining now so up went the hoods and on went the hats. Now they were looking at Woodbarrow. It was decided in view of the weather to perhaps go as far as the Longstone but to then turn back the way they'd come. It looked like the rain was going to be heavier than forecast and was set in for the day. In a way Hannah was relieved as so far all had gone smoothly and her Godmother was quite happy. And then it happened….

On leaving Woodbarrow and all walking in a straight line towards the ever nearing Longstone menhir, the mist swept in accompanied by gusty winds that seemed to hit from all directions. Hannah found she could not see her feet, and nor could anyone else. Heads down against the rain they all kept walking. Hannah realised she should have reached the Longstone by now so she asked her guardian if they were going in the right direction but he didn't respond. Hannah stopped dead in her tracks. She heard her name being called and made off in that direction. Then there came shouts which she tried to follow but the wind blew the sound in all directions.

The Longstone Menhir on Exmoor

Hannah was running hither and thither towards the party but in actual fact she was becoming more and more lost and wandering farther from them.

The rain grew heavier and was now running down her neck and inside her waxed jacket soaking her thoroughly. She stood still in her tracks waiting but not a sound came. Water began to cover her boots and she quickly had to back track away from this boggy area. She had a job to do so because for a moment everywhere she stepped seemed to want to suck her boots off. She made for a fence to find solid ground on which to step safely. The mist lifted slightly but she still couldn't see enough to make out in which direction the Longstone stood as imposing as it was, 9ft above the ground with a smaller one beside it, 'mother and child' her guardian called it. Hannah loved the small watery pool it stood in with all its magical reflections and she longed to be there now.

Hannah came across what appeared to be improved land where horses grazed contentedly. 'Perhaps a farm is close by', she thought to herself, as she approached the horses carefully. As she drew closer to them she found that they were not domesticated animals at all. Their eyes rolled wildly and they tossed their manes whinnying to then bolt off disappearing into the mist. These were real Exmoor ponies.

"Don't leave me, I wont hurt you, come back!" she told them now quite frightened at the ever thickening mist enveloping her on the moor, with no idea really of where she was treading and suddenly realising just how alone she was. She took a deep breath and decided to plough on before darkness would make it impossible to see where on earth she was going. It was going to be a race against time. Now as the wind swept the rains in great shadowy sheets, the atmosphere was truly ghostly. Hannah felt watched. Sometimes she felt as though someone was standing behind her but when she turned about she was merely faced with a blanket of white foreboding mist. She would have to walk faster as she was now soaked to the skin and cold. Should she take off her sodden coat and over trousers she wondered as the wet fabric became stiff and actually quite hard work to move in? She was about to do so in order to move along faster but then she suddenly remembered her guardian warning her of hypothermia. Hannah decided it would be better to keep the layers on and struggle as best she could. She was already cold and shivering.

About half an hour later, movement penetrated the mist. Hannah froze in her tracks. Perhaps the wild Exmoor Beast was lurking nearby. Hannah didn't fancy meeting face to face with a black leopard just now and icicles of fear trembled down her spine. It was raining harder now and the mist was lifting slowly. She was now standing at the top of what appeared to be a deep coomb. Listening she heard water. 'If I can just follow that water down away from the source, it'll lead me to the sea and surely I'll find inhabitation along the way,' she thought. The way down was steep and everywhere she stepped was too boggy to put a foot down properly. Hannah despaired. There was no way on earth she could get near the source of water to follow it down stream. There was nothing for it but to back track. She'd have to try something else.

And now there was more movement through the mist. Not one creature but several all walking in a straight line. The mist lifted just enough for Hannah to make out quite a lot of sheep but why on earth were they walking in a straight line? Hannah loved tales of folklore and recalled her guardian telling her about Ley Lines, the magnetic lines of energy that surround the Earth's circumference. He told her that people of yesteryear often used the ancient stones that marked these Ley Lines for healing because the energy was good. He said that some were nodal stones and not all could be used for healing. Hannah listened to these stories with great interest. It made sense that many creatures would use the Earth's magnetic pull as well as the stars to navigate migratory routes. For a minute Hannah was in a world of her own, her head full of ideas. Were these sheep following a Ley Line? Hannah decided to follow them quietly. After all, they could also be making their way to a farm to be fed. The sheep were weary of her at first but since Hannah made no sudden movements and she kept her distance they soon accepted her presence. A few moments later, and much to Hannah's astonishment, the sheep led her to a small standing stone, and then another and another. Hannah wished she could see the length of the stone row, it was not one she knew from her rambles on Exmoor with her new family. She was cold and shivering now. Hannah held the middle stone for a while to calm down and to think what to do next. The daylight was dimming. She found herself praying, saying 'if I never get off Exmoor again, at least the stones have given me warmth so thank you for that.' It was true she had felt warmth from the stones and for a minute was comforted by the presence of other creatures. The sheep eyed her as if questioning what she thought she was up to up here on her own wandering the moorland. Slowly they wandered off, back into the misty oblivion as if to tell her she couldn't possibly stay with them so she should sally forth like a good human and go back to her own kind. Hannah was alone again. For a moment she felt utterly defeated but she didn't cry. The horses didn't want to know her, the sheep had abandoned her and there was apparently not a sole on Earth anymore. That's how she felt.

Then she decided that there'd be no harm in trying to 'migrate home' like a bird would do. 'Perhaps I can follow a Ley Line,' she thought deciding that everything led somewhere and that Ley Lines often occurred near water since water is a good conductor of electricity. Perhaps she would find a safe stream to follow after all. Hannah had new hope. She took a deep breath and concentrated on the Ley Line as she walked. For a while it seemed to work. She bumped into several stones in the mist and then there were no more. She had a new lease of life now, suddenly getting her second wind. The mist came down again and she had to walk blindly for quite sometime. There were more ponies nearby and something odd through the mist, something white and startling. She couldn't make it out so watching her footing for sinking areas she made her way towards it, straining her eyes through the poor visibility.

Gradually what she was trying to focus on came into view. It was a sheet of white snow and ice on a steep rocky hillside. Hannah found herself looking for cave entrances and somewhere to sleep for the night. She was suddenly cold again and tired. 'Got to keep moving,' she thought as the first signs of hypothermia sent alarm bells running to her brain. She sighed heavily, trying to choose a direction in which to walk. There was a sound she couldn't quite recognise but it seemed to beg her attention. She strained her ears. Perhaps she was hallucinating but she thought she could hear the sound of fresh water tinkling in the distance. She wanted it to be so but could it really be? She listened again moving a little closer. Yes, it was spring water, issuing from the earth. She was at the source of a stream. 'How incredible,' she thought, 'to think that all streams have a source from underground. I wonder if there are oceans of fresh water beneath the Earth's surface.' Hannah's mind drifted away from her task as tiredness hit her over-stressed weary brain. A violent shiver snapped her out of it and she struggled to move her legs. She wasn't pulling her feet out of boggy ground this time either, she was absolutely stiff with cold, having to throw one foot before the other. She flailed her limbs all about in an attempt to get the blood circulating properly and gradually she got herself moving again, cold as she was.

She followed the stream easily for some time. The terrain was solid and she felt safe. In the distance she saw a wide muddy track that looked as though it was used regularly by a farmer so she made for that. 'I'll soon be off the moor,' she thought cheerfully to herself. Just as the muddy track on the distant hillside came into view, Hannah struck a problem. The entire stream was fenced off with barbed wire. The obstruction went in both directions and for a minute Hannah thought it was going to be impossible to cross. Every time she tried to get near, she either couldn't put her hands out because of the barbed wire, or the now danger-ously soggy ground sucked her down. There was no other way. She had to cross this barrier. Now in a state of panic she began worrying what her guardian must be going through wondering what had happened to her. She had to get back before a search party was called. She would never live that humiliation down with her real family! What were her Godmother, uncle and cousins thinking? Surely they'd be furious! Had they got off the moor safely? Hannah was furious with herself. How could such a short pleasant walk in a place she knew by heart have gone so wrong! Well that's the mystery of the moor she decided. It pixie leads people astray for the shear fun of it. 'You haven't beaten me yet Exmoor!' she shouted out in her frustration.

She couldn't stand there all day wondering what to do. The mist had now cleared quite well and the awful oppressiveness had gone with it, though darkness was falling swiftly. In the distance she could see the menacing white swirls of mist dancing it's 'here's where you want to be but not really' dance. She decided to run and leap at the barrier, forgo her hands to the barbed wire and get out of it. If she did it quickly enough she could swing her legs up and over, away from the boggy ground to not get sucked down. If she did it right she'd only come away with a scratch or two. Well that was the plan. She had only one chance to get it right. She also realised that probably a land owner had fenced off his land so wandered if she was now trespassing, or had she been trespassing? She didn't know but she knew she'd be in trouble if she was. She'd better move swiftly.

With a running leap she caught hold of the barrier only to find that the barbed wire did not cut her hands after all, she had actually grabbed on to a wooden structure behind it that she hadn't seen properly before. She swung her legs up but her slippery mud clogged boots hit the wet wire and with an almighty 'squish' her feet hit the ground. With sheer grit and deter-mination, she pulled herself up by her arms, managing to swing her leg high enough to grip the barrier by the heel of her boot. As Hannah pulled herself laboriously over, the barrier moved beneath her just a little for the ground beneath it was wet and loose. She straddled the top of the barrier wondering what she would land into if she let go. She'd have to chance it and decided she could always use the barrier to pull herself up and out if she struck a bog. With no choice in the matter she braced herself for the worse and let go with gritted teeth only to land on solid ground safely the other side. 'How did that happen?' she wondered in disbelief so sure she would sink up to her neck. Without further ado she raced away before fickle Exmoor could change its mind. Hannah encountered a few boggy places where she now trod. What was she doing why was this happening? She had to take stock quickly and soon made the decision that she was far too close to the stream. Swiftly she headed further up the slope away from it, but still able to keep sight of her guiding light of a stream. Hannah now felt she was fighting Exmoor. This was a challenge and the challenge kept her on the move.

Eventually she was able to venture down to the stream and leapt across it to reach the other side. Having issued from its source the steam was still not particularly wide. Hannah was able to leap it with ease and now that track, that lovely used, wide muddy track, was in view close by and accessible. 'Thank God,' thought Hannah and she truly meant it.

Hannah ran up that track so sure she would meet with a house immediately but she did not. 'Always an extra bit to do,' she thought. The track ran steadily upwards and on reach-ing the top of the incline she was able to observe a rather grand house in the distance with its Georgian windows. The ground now facing her looked like a grand park or estate of some kind. 'There's bound to be someone here,' she thought but on approaching the house was devoid of lights and she just knew on-one was home. As she clambered over fallen conifers and other obstacles now physically exhausted more than mentally, for the first time she wept. She'd made it off the moorland. Now she had to find a telephone. Not able to access a clear way through to the big house she looked for the first possible accessible route to any sure sign of human habitation. When she found a way through she was overjoyed. There were farm out buildings, a yard all very promising until she encountered sign after sign of 'trespassers will be prosecuted' and 'keep out.' What now? She had wild imaginings of strange mad old men with shot guns, rabid dogs and heaven only knows what else. Poor Hannah, but she had to go on.

For a While it appeared she'd stumbled upon some kind of ghost town. Every building was 'out of bounds' uninhabited and apparently hostile. Hannah was really scared. She walked on expecting at any minute to be shot or ravaged by dogs. It was uncannily quiet. Eventually she found her way to some modern houses where she dared to knock on the door for help. She felt weak, silly, embarrassed.

A small dog barked incessantly when she first rang the bell. The door opened and Hannah could hear the sizzling of dinner being cooked. Goodness she was hungry but far too distressed to eat anything.

"I'm awfully sorry to bother you but I'm lost." She began to say to the kind looking man that opened the door. He looked concerned.

"I don't suppose you could help me phone in to the Black Venus Inn to leave a message that I'm alright? I'm afraid I don't have any money or anything. I can pay you later though," said Hannah sincerely but in a weak humiliated voice.

The man grinned sideways and asked her where she was heading so she told him what had happened.

"I'm not surprised you got lost in this mist. It doesn't give any warning up here on Exmoor you know, just bang and that's it. Still, lucky you're safe. Hang on a minute," he said pushing the door to and calling out to his wife who told him not to be long. He called his dog, a happy little thing that leaped up into the Land Rover eagerly. The little dog made funny doggy noises like yawning as if to say 'you're alright now you know, my master will see you safe.' Hannah felt easier but the man came out of the house with his coat and she panicked. Was he going to leave her to go off and put the cows to bed or something she found herself wandering.

'May I not use your phone Sir?' she asked.

"Ah maid there wont be no-one there now it isn't opening hours yet. I'll pop you back, it'll be easier all round," he said.

"But wont your wife mind?" asked Hannah knowing she was cooking his tea from the sizzling noises.

He made a sort of hearty laugh saying she was used to it and that Hannah wasn't the first to be lost up there on the moor. Hannah felt better and not quite so silly. In fact she couldn't believe her luck and apologised for putting him out.

And oh dear, for now came the sudden realisation of the inevitable confrontation to come. Maybe her guardian wouldn't want her around now after humiliating him by getting lost and maybe his wife wouldn't want Hannah in the house for the same reason. Her Godmother would be sure to say 'you can't stay with your new family now after all this…" Oh what a mess! The man in the Land Rover, a Mr Macracken, was asking a tearful Hannah if she was alright and she hardly knew how to answer him. She stopped crying fearful he'd stop and throw her out for being silly but he did not. How kind he was and so thoughtful, perhaps that's why Hannah was crying, not having realised there were other warm and kind people besides those she knew, her Guardian and possibly her Godmother, though she didn't know for sure if her Godmother would support her, it all hinged on today.

Mr Macracken began to talk about his little dog and that made Hannah feel better, she even managed a smile. The Land Rover swung into the car park. Hannah caught sight of her Godmother sitting alone in her estate car. She guessed the rest of the party must be at Break Neck Hole or somewhere waiting for her just in case she returned that way. Hannah was wandering what to say to her Godmother and stuttering her thanks to Mr Macracken at the same time. He seemed to understand her nervousness even though Hannah had not explained much to him, but he knew people and read them well. He knew Hannah was genuine. He came from Woolhanger and Hannah promised that her guardian would be in touch soon. Mr Macracken was eager to get back for his tea. How kind he was to have gone to all that trouble. Hannah's Godmother gave her a hearty hug saying she was trying to work out what on earth to tell Hannah's mother who would have had a field day with all this so thank goodness she was back safe and sound. It was decided not to say anything at all to her mother, seeing as all was well now. She would have to persuade her husband, Hannah's uncle, to do the same. Now Hannah knew her Godmother really cared about her, what a relief.

Soon the rest of the party were reunited in the car park with hugs all round and all was well. It was decided Hannah had proven herself and 'had her head well screwed on' under the circumstances and yes, of course her new guardian still wanted her, so all was well. Tea and a hot bath on returning home put paid to her shivers, though it was several days before her nerves truly calmed down again. Never again would Hannah venture out onto Exmoor without a compass, map and at least change for the telephone, if not a mobile, though Hannah did however, remain 'friends' with the mysterious Exmoor.
Thank you Mr Macracken!

THE END

Magnificent Adventures

Vincent's Magnificent Adventure

Vincent was a quiet lad. He sometimes wandered the countryside looking at birdlife and other wildlife, contented with his own company. Vincent had lots of friends of course but not all were interested in the same countryside pursuits as he was.

One afternoon Vincent decided to explore the Devonshire countryside around and about Triumphal Arch, a stone folly situated high on a hillside with spectacular views for miles around. Vincent had long legs and it didn't take him long to reach the top. He was very fit and didn't huff or puff, so used was he to long excursions. Fumbling in his pocket he pulled out an apple and began to crunch through its crisp skin. He caught the juice with his tongue just in time as it ran down his chin. 'Hmmm', he sighed. He did enjoy a good apple.

The folly was a funny structure and he always thought to himself that surely there must be an invisible castle attached to this grand entrance. 'Funny sort of person, to take all the trouble in the World to build where a door might go and then leave off. Perhaps they ran out of money or something,' he thought to himself taking another bite of his apple.

He fumbled in his other pocket to find a small rather useful binocular his father had given him recently for his birthday. The binocular was Vincent's most prized possession and he smiled happily every time he used them. From the top of the hill and leaning on the folly he could see clearly across to the estuary, various hedgerows and fields, all good places as wildlife habitat. He bird watched for an hour or so quite forgetting the time. He found a robin's nest close by and was careful not to disturb the parents from feeding their young ones. A buzzard mewed over head but the estuary birds were inaudible here and most had gone off to breed. He watched the lumbering flight of wood pigeons, heard the low whistle of a blackbird's alarm call followed by it's 'pink, pink, pink', call as a magpie bothered its family but all was well and both parent blackbirds saw the magpie off in no uncertain terms. The birds began to go to roost singing their prayers before they settled down properly. Now the ears of rabbits began to pop up here and there in the fields as the afternoon drew to a

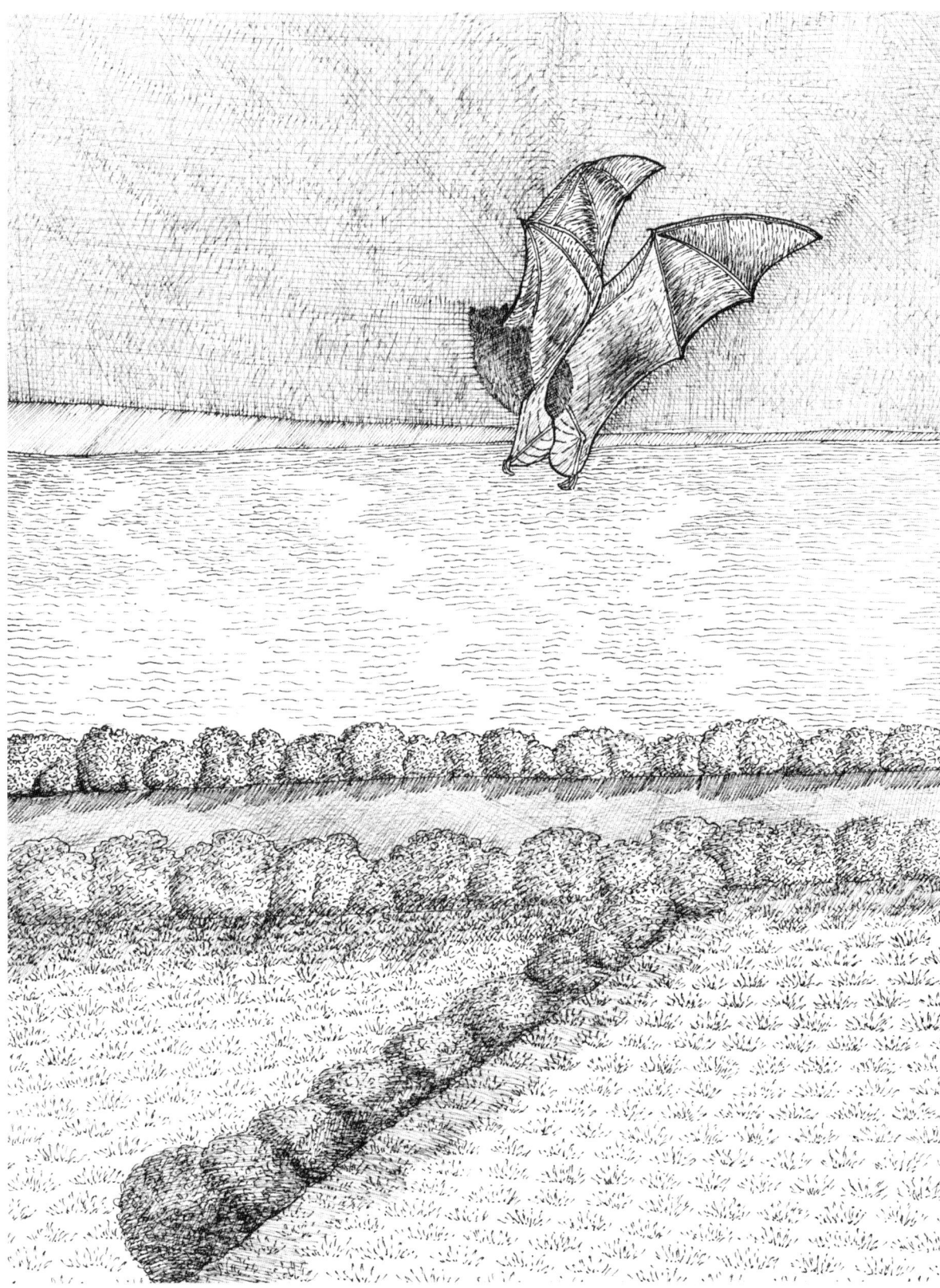

Vincent in bat form heading for the Taw Estuary!

close and the light slowly faded. 'Bother,' said Vincent knowing it was time for home.

Then, as he turned about, there was a 'swish' as a bat brushed passed his ear. It flew quite differently compared with the birds he'd been watching and he knew instinctively that he was observing our only British flying mammal. Well naturally, Vincent was delighted but knowing he had to get home now, he happened to say aloud to the bat:

"Oh if only I could be a bat for just one night! I could learn all about you."

Well little did Vincent realise but he was actually standing inside a fairy ring. It was so large a fairy ring that Vincent hadn't really taken much notice of the circle of mushrooms hidden in the grass. Suddenly a pretty little fairy dressed in a flowing green and silver tunic stepped out from behind the largest mushroom and said:

"If that is your true wish dear Vincent you shall have it for you are a good boy." She made a motion with her hand and suddenly he was illuminated in a moon beam. The shadows grew fast now across the fields, the folly was but a silhouette and…. Oh what was this! It was becoming larger and larger. Actually Vincent was becoming smaller and smaller but it wasn't until he became really very hairy that he realised what was happening. For a minute he panicked waving his wings this way and that and before the fairy could instruct him he was suddenly on the wing.

"Oh heavens I can't fly!" He called.

"Vincent come back, I haven't taught you how to…….." called the fairy but it was no good. Vincent was gone.

Truly he was the most ungainly bat you've ever seen because he couldn't yet fly properly. He flew over the hedgerows with little coordination and soon found himself hurtling far too fast towards a huge tree or something he couldn't quite see. The darkness enveloped the whole place and suddenly visibility was poor. His own eyesight was better than this in the dark! Heavens what should he do? He seemed to be flying into oblivion and Vincent found himself screaming "aaaaaaah!"

It was an odd thing to happen but upon screaming Vincent found that his ears tickled and felt different. Little did he realise that now he was in bat form he'd acquired a fleshy spike in each ear called a 'tragus'. A tragus is an important part of a bat's sound reception system. He wiggled his ears and shook his head. That was better and now Vincent's bat instincts were beginning to take over. So now when he cried out he moved his head from side to side instinctively. Upon doing so, Vincent's cries acted like a radar system, like on a ship or in an aeroplane. Supersonic vibrations echoed from obstacles before him and he was soon able to navigate his way about. This was echo-location and exactly how real bats navigate. However, as soon as he stopped calling out his new found in-built radar system stopped working so he had to make a lot of noise. Vincent was really enjoying himself but was still trying to get his wings to coordinate properly, after all it was his first go at flying, and no mean feat.

Before long Vincent the bat was zooming awkwardly across the Tarka Trail, close by Heanton. A man and his son were walking with their dog and Vincent guessed they must be bat or badger watching or something like that. 'Naturalists' he thought as both carried binoculars.

"Hey Dad look! That's a funny sort of bat isn't it? I've never seen one fly like that before," said the boy, pointing up but Vincent never heard the reply. He was long gone and away over the estuary now.

Vincent was still laughing when suddenly he had a problem. He was losing height and becoming dangerously close to the Taw Estuary's surface. Vincent shouted and shouted. He could sense exactly the trouble ahead but no amount of echo-location would help him steer his wings properly. A great tit was disturbed from her roost and swans took to the wing in fright as Vincent accidentally brushed by them. Here came the water and in he would go with a loud 'plop!' Vincent cringed and that altered his wing shape. His eyes were tightly shut but he soon realised that he should have hit the water long ago but here he still was all dry. He'd actually zoomed clear of the water and now found that by tilting his wings up he could alter his direction. Now he could navigate! He practised his wings to flutter in this direction and that. He was really having fun. Not a soul, not even an expert would be able to tell him apart from the normal pipistrelle bats now. "I am a bat!" he shouted happily.

A loud hoot sent shivers down his spine. He wondered why. He loved owls. Large moths fluttered about and instinctively he caught one. 'Crunch!' For a minute Vincent was surprised at himself wondering what he did that for but then he was a bat after all. The presence of the large hairy moth in his mouth wasn't at all unpleasant. So he ate it finding it to be actually quite nice, although he decided it definitely wasn't something he was going to try once he was a person again.

"Hooo hooooo!" called the owl again launching itself from a twisty ancient oak. Vincent thought it was a beautiful tawny owl until he realised it was after him in the same way as he'd been after the moth. Now he was being predated!

"Good Lord," he thought "what shall I do?"

There was nothing for it but to out fly this mighty predator.

"Whoosh!" went the owl's talons past Vincent's furry ears. Vincent flew faster. He was up around Ashford now zig-zagging around the large hedgerow trees to eventually drop down into a dell where he kept extremely still and made not a sound. The owl perched near by watching and listening intently for the slightest sound. Vincent picked up an earthen clod. He threw it away from him to make a decoy. It worked. The owl dropped down onto the earthen clod and then took to the wing once again, defeated. It screamed defiantly and was gone. Vincent was trembling with fear. He'd come very close to being eaten and was almost too afraid to move.

Somewhere in the distance a fox came running fast as lightning to where Vincent huddled hidden in the grass. Vincent could hear its foot falls. Was he being predated again he wondered? Should he fly up into the trees and out of harms way? Somehow Vincent's instincts kicked in and he remained where he was. A tiny voice was calling his name.

"Vincent, Vincent! Are you alright?" came the shouts of the frantic green and silver clad fairy.

"Oh goodness, we came as fast as we could but I really do think that that's quite enough for one night. I think I should change you back into a boy before you encounter any real harm!" Decided the fairy and Vincent agreed even though he had quite enjoyed being a bat for a while, especially the flying part.

The fairy waved her arms and chanted some magical fey words. Suddenly Vincent was once again illuminated in moonshine. His nose began to tickle rather terribly and he sneezed violently. In the next instant Vincent's charm had worn off and he was a person again.

"Thank you so much." He said to the fairy.

"Just remember Vincent, be careful what you dream, for dreams really can come true." The fairy whispered to him and then,

"Come Lady Fern," she said to her foxy friend and off they sped, back to the folly to leap back into the magical fairy ring never to be seen again. Wow!

"Vincent! Vincent!" called a voice.

Oh heavens that was his father. "Where are you boy?"

Vincent ran to his father and gave him a hug.

"Gosh am I glad to be a person again!" he said not thinking what he was saying.

"What are you on about? You got bats in the belfry lad?"

"No father." Said Vincent laughing and thinking his father couldn't have said anything more appropriate under the circumstances.

"Your Mother said you were up here. You're late for your supper so I said I'd fetch you home. Next birthday I'm getting you a watch but ah….. well……. I'm glad you're alright." His father told him forgiving him.

Vincent was so glad to ride home in the car because his arms really ached after all that flying about.

"You must be hungry. Your Mother said you were gone hours." Said his father sounding concerned.

Well Vincent refrained from saying what he almost said which would have been, 'oh I was fine I ate an apple and a moth which was most satisfying, thank you,' and said instead that he was hungry. He also promised to take greater care not to be late again. He didn't like to trouble his worrying parents. He was after all a good boy and all good boys and girls respect their parents.

THE END

Anne's Magnificent Adventure

Anne had promised to look after the goats just until her mother returned from shopping. It was Saturday and Anne was enjoying her day home from school. Her two tabby cats, Tigger and Tansy were playing about chewing the tassels that were dangling from a throw covering the sofa. They liked a good game but were somehow always naughtier when Anne was at home alone with them. She'd just had her twelfth birthday and was enjoying her bit of independence when occasionally left home to do homework or relax. It was good to feel responsible, there was a nice grown up feeling about it.

It was a lovely day. The sun streamed in through the old rectory windows lighting the table she was working on, arranging flowers in an oasis for her Grandmother's birthday tomorrow. Anne was good with things like that. She had a real feel for plants and a deep interest in what they were about. She'd been allocated a special herb patch in the garden and intended to plant up her little patch of bare earth tomorrow. Anne was hoping her mother would bring her back a small pot of chives. It was the one plant missing from her birthday collection. She was already planning the layout in her head. Tall plants at the back, short ones at the front, her Grandmother had advised her.

While Anne was busy in her head the goats were, as always, looking for mischief. They loved attention and had discovered that if they chewed in the right place at the right time, they could sometimes escape and have their owners dashing about in a wonderful game of tag, sometimes for hours. Truly it was marvellous to watch the expressions on a persons' face, particularly when the intended quarry was only just out of reach. Oh the delights of being a goat. What fun they had and since today was such a lovely day well, there was no harm in trying for another game of tag. Anne wouldn't mind after all, she was such a good natured girl.

The clever goats were chewing rapidly through the new rope that Anne's father had only just put on the day before, and that held the gate fast. They chewed with such zest that the wooden five barred gate rattled slightly, inaudible to Anne yet perfectly audible to Tigger and Tansy who immediately pricked up their ears.

"Meow!" They cried in unison.

Anne thought they wanted to be let out so she opened the door but forgot to look in the direction of the goat paddock. The cats cried again after the door was closed behind them. Anne laughed telling them to make their minds up, "in or out?" she asked them.

Suddenly there was a 'thump!' The gate to the goat paddock flew open bumping the old stone wall as it swung and out marched the two naughty goats.

"Look at us Tigger and Tansy, aren't we marvellous. We've done it again!" They bleated skipping off in the direction of a startled pheasant that took to the wing calling 'Coch, coch, coch!'

Anne looked up just in time to see their wagging tails disappearing off into the distance.

"Oh no!" she cried grabbing her wellington boots and jacket.

Within minutes Anne was running as fast as she could so as not to lose sight of the goats. They were wandering up through the trees, following a path made by red deer that was so much easier to walk on rather than directly through the dense undergrowth. A leisurely nibble here and a nibble there with tails wagging as the naughty goats bleated their excitement. What fun they were having.

Anne followed the sound of their bleating, not running now for fear she would have them running off at full pelt. This strange walk chase continued on for some time until they were right at the top of Poleshill Lane. Now Anne found they were heading in the direction of the folly known as Triumphal Arch. Something attracted the goats to go on. It was almost as if they were being lured by something. It wasn't until Anne reached the top and glanced across at Triumphal Arch that she realised it was aglow with a strange radiant light. Soft rain seemed to drip off a glass structure directly behind the arch that Anne had never seen before and when the sun shone directly upon it, there were bright flashes of every colour of the rainbow rather like those that shine from the facets of a crystal. Something magical was happening. This was a true Crystal Palace but to whom it belonged Anne had no idea. There was not a soul around, most people keeping in doors and avoiding the drizzling rain Anne suspected. For a moment she watched in awe.

Alarmingly Anne noticed all sorts of animals heading for the strange light radiating from the palace including hedgehogs, deer, rabbits and her goats! Whatever was happening? Anne simply had to investigate. She could feel her adrenalin rushing through her insides like lots of butterflies in some mad dance. Butterflies were good to have in your tummy, according to Anne's Grandmother, because they kept one cautious and alert. "Anne, you'll never be over confident if you have a few butterflies from time to time." She had told her. Anne's Grandfather had been in the Navy and always swore by butterflies, saying that once he and his best friend went off to fight for his country on a mission. It was the first time his friend hadn't had butterflies and that was the day he was killed. Anne wasn't sure why she was remembering all this now for it had been advice given to her before sitting a test at school when she had been particularly nervous. Grandparents always had a way of making you put things into perspective somehow. She always did her best but she wasn't going to be killed in a war if she did badly at her assessment and nerves would sharpen her mind. Now, she was being challenged again. Her mother had asked her to look after the goats so it was important to find them, take them home and show her mother how responsible she could be. If Anne could get the goats home before her Mother returned from shopping then she need never know they had escaped. 'Right,' thought Anne positively. 'That's what I'm going to do.'

Two naughty goats

Anne ventured closer to her goats. If she could just get a little nearer she might just be able to reach their collars. It was to no avail. Anne stepped on a small twig that cracked under her wellington boots and off went the goats once again, leading her a right merry dance. After a while Anne stopped in her tracks and sighed but as she was staring at her boots wondering what to do next, she heard a tiny voice. The odd thing is as small as the voice was she was absolutely sure that her goats bleated responses! How could that possibly be? Who were her goats talking to? Anne crept a little closer and to her astonishment caught sight of a small gnome. His beard was as wild as the wild clematis all gone to seed. His jacket and trousers were a smart green. He wore ivy wood carved clogs and had a funny hat. The hat was in the same fabric and colour as his suit but in a sort of Robin Hood style and it had a Jay's feather stuck in the side of it. The gnome appeared to be selling tokens to the animals yet how the animals were paying for the tokens and what they were for was anyone's guess.

Anne decided to watch and see what she could find out.

"Roll up, roll up, get your tokens here!" The gnome yelled.

Two squirrels sprang towards him having descended from the hedgerow. They nosed forwards two sprigs of hawthorn berries, called haws, which the gnome accepted. The squirrels were presented with one golden token each and on they bounded towards the ever flashing crystal palace.

Now badgers came to the gnome, bringing with them fresh hay bedding that they had acquired from the farmers barn up the lane. That was accepted and the badgers were given gold tokens. Anne watched them scurry away to follow the squirrels.

Two young hedgehogs were leading along an old blind hedgehog. They were cheekily putting berries on his spines to save them carrying them. The poor old hedgehog's spines were almost full!

"So it's one of those human shopping trolley's I am is it eh! Lol, a shopping trolley hog be I, Lol" the old hedgehog was chuckling.

The hedgehogs had seen shopping trolley's used in the garden centre but using their spines to carry items was an age old hog trick. The old hedgehog enjoyed stirring up a bit of troublesome fun. When the gnome had pulled the last of the berries from the old hog's spines Anne heard them saying as they disappeared across the field,

"Right then Granfer, when your legs don't work any more we'll get you some wheels as well, just like one of those trolley things."

"Get me some wheels…. Oh ho ho!"

Next in line were Anne's two goats. They presented the gnome with hazel sprigs heavily laden with nuts. The gnome had a job to take the hazel leaves away for the goats were nibbling at them all the time. Reluctantly the goats parted with the hazel sprigs and the gnome handed over the tokens. Anne wondered whatever she could give the gnome. She needed to see where the goats were going. She reached inside her pocket to find a half eaten chocolate bar, a bit of old string and a clean handkerchief. She wasn't sure they were suitable to give the gnome so she began collecting rose hips, beech mast and acorns. Anne waited her turn which was after three wood mice had handed in grass seed and a fourth suddenly appeared with sun flower seed.

"Where did you get that?" squeaked the first mouse.

"Well, I got them from a bird food table in a garden just up the lane. There are peanuts too but I couldn't carry any more." replied the fourth mouse.

All the mice giggled and were suddenly away across the field to join the other animals.

Anne approached the gnome who was astounded to see a person. His name was Jack by the Hedge, after the wild garlic plant, and in any case he always conducted any business he had to do standing by a hedge. He politely tipped his cap and bowed to her.

"Oh, my name is Anne. I was hoping to fetch my goats. They broke lose from the paddock you see and I must get them home before my mother returns but now they seem to have gone off with the other animals." Anne explained.

Jack by the Hedge nodded. He couldn't refuse Anne a token because she had politely complied with the rules but he warned her that she would be the only human to join in the fun.

"What fun?" Anne wanted to know.

The surprised gnome stared at her before replying, "Why the Green Fairy's birthday party of course! I'm surprised you haven't been before, there are three parties every year."

"Do you mean that the Green Fairy has three birthday parties every year all for herself?" Anne gasped in astonishment.

"Why yes, yes I do indeed!" laughed the gnome adding "she can do just as she pleases, she is Queen of the Triumphal Arch Fairy Tribe. As I recall, one year she had five birthdays."

"Heavens!" Anne exclaimed and just as she was about to ask another question the gnome vanished but his voiced echoed for her to hurry.

Anne picked up her gold token and ran across the field to catch up with the other animals that were swiftly disappearing from view.

It was a strange thing to be able to hear the animals talking. Some squirrels were talking about a leaky drey they needed to sort out before bed time and another invited them to come to her drey until the roof was fixed. Then it was decided that there wouldn't be enough room to all roost in the same one. Another squirrel remembered a buzzard box being erected in a large garden. Since there were no buzzards using it, it was decided the squirrels could move into that instead.

Some wood mice were talking about the difficulty of storing grass seed during mild winters since if it isn't bone dry it tends to go mouldy. A fat mouse squeaked that he had a perfect answer for that problem… 'Eat it!' There was a lot of laughter for he was only teasing and knew jolly well how important it was to store food for winter.

The red deer were saying they'd be moving on up to Exmoor soon as that's where the rutt takes place. A little brown rat was running around taking bets as to who would win. "Come along now, come along, it's all for charity…" The rat had a funny way of talking through his nose and sniffing around each creature he approached.

The badgers were subdued. They were speaking quietly of an elderly Grand-badger who was doddering around these days and terribly forgetful. They were saying he had great difficulty now in changing his bed so they'd have to do it for him on the next sunny day, pull all the bedding out, air it in the sun and then push it all back in again. As they were planning all this Anne realised just how like people the animals were with all their struggles and worries or rather just how animal-like people were. Indeed people are animals and part of Nature. Are we really *better* than animals? Certainly we are more destructive in digging up wild habitats she was thinking. *Better?* That was a funny word. Perhaps some people are better than other people she decided. After all, a caring person was surely better than a non-caring person.

The Crystal Palace was magnificently beautiful. A fairy clad in autumnal colours greeted the animals, taking their tokens whilst another ushered them away inside. Anne followed. It was rather like walking through mist at first and most of the animals held each others tails, a bit like elephants do so as not to lose each other. Soon they were inside the palace and were asked to make themselves comfortable. They gathered around a huge crystal stadium and all wished the Green Fairy a happy birthday upon which there was much tail banging. Gifts were gathered by the attendants and placed on a mossy table by an exquisite water fountain where the animals were allowed to drink should they become thirsty. Anne pulled out her clean handkerchief with the embroidered ferns on and handed it to one of the attendants realising it would make a perfect table cloth for the Green Fairy. She would be pleased!

After the introductory birthday speech, Jack by the Hedge arrived to thank the animals for their support. As it turned out every birthday party the Green Fairy had, served as a charity Gala. This time the Gala was in aid of the 'Help the Aged Wildlife Charity'. All the produce received, in return for gold tokens to the gala, would be handed out over the next month by the Triumphal Arch Fairy Tribe, in order to see the elderly wildlife that had no-one to look after them surviving the coming winter. There was a big cheer, more tail banging, and then the musical event began.

Anne had never seen a musical event quite like it. It was called 'Nature'. All the musical notes were produced from rain, wind gusting or howling, dew drops, fungi spores exploding into the wind, seed pods bursting, seeds scattering, blackbirds scratching through leaves, and before each one was shown on the screen you had to guess what it was that made each sound, then it was all put together like a strange symphony with the climax, the crescendo, being thunder and lighting to finish dramatically. At that moment the two goats caught sight of Anne and tried to hide under her coat, glad she was there because they didn't like thunder. Luckily they were wearing their collars so Anne put them on their leashes. The music ceased marking the end of the Gala. The moment the leashes were fastened and the goats were safe by her side, mist enveloped them all. Anne was wondering what to ask her goats seeing as they could speak now but just as she was about to ask them something, she suddenly found herself back outside, beside Triumphal Arch with no fairies, no Jack by the Hedge, no wild animals, just herself and the goats.

"Bleeeeat," they said in unison, and all was back to normal.

Anne noticed a huge fairy ring of mushrooms surrounding them. "How lovely," she thought stepping out to find the nearby Poleshill Lane.

On arriving home, Anne's mother had just arrived and caught sight of her walking back up to the house with the two goats.

"Aren't you good taking them for a walk. I've tried many times to get them to walk by my side, fancy you managing that. Oh Anne, you are a wonderful daughter." said her mother unloading the shopping from the car boot.

Anne felt very proud and yes, the goats did respect Anne and they'd think twice about breaking out again just in case it thundered and she wasn't there to comfort them. Her adventure had seemed so dream-like. It certainly was not an adventure a grown-up would believe in and Anne knew she'd have to keep it to herself. A secret she and her goats would keep although she may decide to share it with Tigger and Tansy at bedtime.

THE END

Tess & Andrew's Magnificent Adventure

Tess was quietly listening to her iPod in the back of her parents' Land Rover. Her father drove quite smoothly and she was enjoying the scenery and treed tunnels they travelled through. The dappled shade and sunlight was so pretty on this quiet road. Tess knew her parents would be talking about boring business matters again. She watched their head movements and gestures. How busy they were. Today was an important day. Her father was going to meet an old contact he'd recently become reacquainted with only to find they both had similar freelance businesses, although each specialised in separate fields. The idea was to talk about setting up a proper company. If this deal went well they would be moving up to Devon from Cornwall permanently and Tess would have to leave her friends behind. In truth Tess was as anxious about this meeting as her parents were but it was also rather exciting.

The Land Rover slowed as they reached the 30 miles per hour sign. She heard the tick-tick ticking of the indicator as the vehicle swung left turning into Muddiford Inn's car park. Tess turned her iPod off as her mother said it was anti-social to be listening to it when introduced to new friends. Several cars were already parked up. Then Tess's father said
"Oh look they're here! Over in the garden sat in the sun."
Tess looked across to see a smart middle aged couple talking together.
"I thought they were bringing Andrew? I think it's important the children meet as well." Remarked her mother disappointedly.
As it turned out they had brought their son Andrew along but apparently he'd gone off bird watching and would be back at 1pm to join them for lunch.
"There's a lovely woodland walk just up along the side of the Inn. Andrew wont have gone far. Why don't you go and look for him Tess?" Suggested Andrew's mother and all agreed that was a good idea. The grown ups wanted to talk and Tess would be glad to leave them to it so off she went.

Devon felt different to Cornwall somehow though Tess couldn't quite fathom out why. She walked along the dried mud lane and enjoyed the lush trees and wild flowers. It was a beautiful day and Tess breathed in the sweet Devonshire air, so different to the fresh salty air of

The Muddiford Inn

her Cornish fishing village where she lived. Eventually she came to a clearing and sat down to admire a red deer cautiously watching her. Squirrels played about, they always made her laugh. Nature's little clowns dashing here and there she thought, and a woodmouse poked about the hedge rummaging for whatever it could find to eat. How peaceful. So much more peaceful than her home-life with her hard working parents never ceasing to chat about new ideas and the next business plan to achieve, or the next presentation to the bank or the next potential client they would be having to lunch. Tess had a high respect for her parents but she was quite often lonely.

For a moment, Tess caught sight of something moving at the base of a huge beech tree. She giggled to herself for she could have sworn it was just like a little man. When she strained her eyes to see there was absolutely nothing. 'You're losing it Tess,' she told herself. Suddenly the deer darted away and she heard footsteps in the opposite direction, coming up along the trail towards her. There was a tall gangly legged fellow approaching her.

"Hello I'm Andrew." He said holding out his hand to shake hers. Rising Tess shook hands and introduced herself. He told her all about the birds he'd seen that day including a sparrowhawk that had made a kill, lots of small birds in the cherry orchard, and a woodpecker. Clearly Andrew was knowledgeable on bird life. They chatted about iPods and computers as well and very soon it was time to head back to Muddiford Inn for lunch. Tess was so relieved that Andrew was 'normal' for she had imagined him quite unapproachable and better than herself. Both were on equal terms. The two families would be spending a lot of time together so it was inevitable that Tess and Andrew would be seeing a great deal of each other if their parents merged their businesses. Both Tess and Andrew had been worried but now things seemed a little easier.

Andrew put on a posh voice which made Tess laugh as both families had Westcountry accents but a business voice was sometimes acquired for the telephone and such.

"Well, shall we go for lunch Miss." He said and both got the giggles all the way back to the Inn.

Lunch up in the restaurant was amazing. Tess had never had such fabulous food but the business talk continued. Later when they were sitting in the old part of the Inn, in the lounge/bar area for coffee everyone was feeling deeply satisfied after their meal. Tensions were lessened and it appeared the talks were going well. Tess was relaxed and half daydreaming into her drink when something caught her eye. She looked up to find nothing. Then she heard a small voice humming merrily. Glancing across the room she saw a small girl wearing a daisy chain, drawing at one of the tables all alone. Tess smiled at her and the little girl smiled back holding up her drawing of a woodmouse.

"Oh that's lovely," exclaimed Tess upon which the child vanished!

"What's lovely Tess?" Asked her mother.

"You alright love? You've suddenly lost your colour." Her father said.

"You look like you've seen a ghost!" Andrew added.

Everyone was staring at her and Tess felt uncomfortable.

"Do you know, I do believe I have!" Tess exclaimed.

Tess's mother looked angry.

"Oh do excuse her Jean, she'd do this when she was a little girl, you know for attention. Quite understandable given the amount of time we were able to spend with her, poor darling. Do you remember that imaginary friend you used to have?" asked her mother.

Tess looked at her open mouthed but said nothing blushing profusely.

"I had hoped you'd grown out of all that," added her mother in a low voice from the corner of her mouth.

Now her father chipped in to save the day.

The Ghostly Child

"What a superb way to get our daughter's colour back. Embarrass the poor lass." He said winking at Tess and she felt instantly better but was aching to get away.

Soft laughter made light of the situation but Andrew's mum felt how uncomfortable Tess was.

"Have you tried Andrew's binocular dear? They're very good," she said, giving Tess a wink and an excuse to escape.

"Er, no actually I haven't." Tess replied.

"Brilliant idea, Tess love, you need a hobby," said her mother.

And with that Tess and Andrew escaped back out into the lovely large garden of Muddiford Inn to try out Andrew's binocular. Tess soon got the hang of them but as they were bird watching, Andrew suddenly froze. Tess followed his gaze to see the little daisy chain girl mysteriously drifting, through a newer part of 16th Century Coaching Inn.

"You can see her? Tell me you can see her too!" Tess begged.

"I can, I truly can!" Andrew replied describing her to Tess and adding,

"Come on, let's follow her and see what she does."

The daisy chain ghost drifted along out from the other side of the Inn, heading for the Woodland walk where Tess and Andrew had been before lunch. The Woodland walk wasn't accessible from the garden. They'd have to double back and hope not to lose sight of the ghostly child or they'd never find out where she was going or what she was doing. Of course there was a chance she would just vanish into thin air, just as she had done lunch time. Tess wondered if they'd be lucky enough to glimpse her again. She felt no fear at all merely a peaceful benevolence.

So, Andrew and Tess had to go back around the Inn in order to reach the woodland walkway. Both their parents were now sitting in the patio area chatting when Tess's mother called out,

"Tess I owe you an apology, the owner was saying the Inn is actually haunted. I must say I find it all most extraordinary…."

"Not now mother I'm busy," Tess called back to her now open mouthed mother, who was actually pleasantly surprised, and she and Andrew raced away so as not to lose sight of the daisy chain ghost.

"I can't believe I've just told my mother that *I'm* too busy to talk to her." Tess exclaimed to Andrew and they both laughed.

Once on the woodland walk, for a moment they thought they'd lost their quarry. Then, a gentle humming drew their attention to the cherry orchard where the child was 'drifting' up the bank to reach the wooded area. She then drifted through various trees, holding her drawing firmly in her small hand. Perhaps the trees had been in other places when the child had been alive. She was actually a beautiful child and hummed the whole way along the trail until she reached the open area surrounded by beech trees where Tess had sat earlier. Tess and Andrew kept their distance so as not to startle her. Both were excited and in awe of the situation. Their hearts pounded in the anticipation of what was to come. Never before had either experienced a paranormal event like this though both had read about such things in ghost stories and comics. Up until now it had all been merely fun or a thrilling read but now something was really happening.

The daisy chain ghost arrived at the largest beech tree with a little hollow in the bottom.

"Hello!" she called softly.

"Arrh, Evelyn!" cried a gruff voice.

Out from the tree came a little man as gnarled as the old tree. He had a kind face but was clearly a goblin.

"What have you there my pretty little friend," he said to the child reaching out for her drawing.

She handed it over silently and he examined it.

"Arrh, so you've drawn a woodmouse today. The ears aren't quite right and its tail is too long but all in all a very good little mouse. You are getting good aren't you!" said the goblin praising her and re-drawing certain parts of her mouse to show her what to do next time. Evelyn clapped her hands excitedly when she saw the drawing finished.

"Oh yes, that's better. Now he looks real!" she said humming and doing a mouse-like little dance.

"Arrh so it's a 'he' is it? Well you must draw a 'she' mouse tomorrow so that he can have a friend. Now then, what have you called him?" asked the goblin looking at her with twinkly eyes.

"Oh, erm, well I thought he should be called Woody because he's a wood mouse and then tomorrow when I've drawn his wife, she can be called Fern because ferns like to grow in woods don't they Mr Goblin?" Evelyn announced all in an excited rush.

"That's right child, among other places. Now are you ready?" he asked.

"Oh yes, yes, please do it!" said the child clapping her hands and jumping up and down excitedly. Her ghostly form seeming so much more solid now noticed Andrew and Tess. They looked on wondering what was going to happen. This was extraordinary!

The goblin picked up a withy stick, pointed it at the drawing and told Evelyn to hold the picture flat on the floor in case the mouse hurt itself.

Tess smiled, what a lovely way to play with the child and help her learn about Nature she thought.

Evelyn announced the paper was getting warm and the goblin said

"Good, good it's working then but be still and quiet now until it's done."

Evelyn nodded and a light radiated from the goblin's withy stick. Next he put his hands over the paper and a mass of rainbow colours seemed to be mixing about with his gestures. The drawing was soon in colour, even the eyes of the little wood mouse glistened with life. It was quite extraordinary. But the magic didn't end there. Now the mouse was taking on form, a body shape and after a few minutes its small fury body began to wriggle. It took a few minutes more and suddenly a real wood mouse was sitting up washing itself on Evelyn's drawing paper, where her sketch had once been. How delighted she was, her small face all aglow in the fading magical light. Now the woodmouse was sat up on its haunches as tall as can be to take a bow to the goblin and one to Evelyn. The goblin picked up his withy stick to touch the mouse once on each shoulder saying.

"We name you Woody King of the Woodmice. May your reign be long, loyal and fair."

With that nine wild woodmice came to take their new king away on a tiny thrown made of beech mast and golden leaves that had been carefully preserved since autumn. They'd be back tomorrow when Evelyn had finished her drawing of another, almost identical wood mouse which would become Woody's Queen. She would be Queen Fern. When all the mice had gone the goblin praised Evelyn and told her now to sleep a while. Evelyn readily agreed so long as the goblin promised to tell her a story first and so that was agreed.

The goblin perched himself on a tree stump. He was less than half her size. He waited until she had made herself comfortable on the woodland floor before beginning his story. As he began to speak, squirrels, birds, mice, voles, deer, foxes and badgers all came about to sit next to Evelyn. The goblin laughed saying he could always tell the wild creatures Evelyn had drawn, the ones he had brought to life for they had a terrible weakness for a good story. But there was no harm in that. Just as the goblin began to speak the child's form began to fade and all the creatures and rainbow colours around her with it. The goblin became part of the tree once more and soon, Evelyn, the daisy chain ghost was gone altogether. Tess and Andrew were sad to see her go. It was almost an anti-climax even though both had been deeply privileged to see her in the first place.

"It just goes to prove that life goes on in many different forms. We've glimpsed another place somewhere haven't we Tess." Andrew said and Tess agreed.

A great tit alighted on a branch over their heads calling "teacher, teacher, teacher". Andrew thought that was appropriate somehow and told Tess so. She thought so too. The goblin was clearly teaching Evelyn how to draw as well as about Nature.

Tess and Andrew agreed to keep their vision to themselves yet Tess couldn't help feeling she was meant to have seen Evelyn.

"Well your mother wanted you to have a hobby. Perhaps Evelyn wants you to take up drawing. You know you're welcome to join me bird watching any time. You could come along and draw birds. My parents usually go somewhere on a Sunday, we keep Sunday's free whatever happens." Andrew told her.

That was the beginning of a long and trusted friendship. In a way it was Evelyn that had taught them to trust each other by giving them a secret to share, her secret. As it turned out Andrew had a lot of friends with sisters and Tess would be going to Secondary School with all of them. For the first time in a long time, Tess and Andrew seemed happy about their future prospects. After all if the company was a success, they'd both have jobs to go to later on and Andrew was quick to point this out, so all was well after their full day.

THE END

Toby's Magnificent Adventure

Toby was a Dachshund. He lived in a beautiful country house in the heart of Devonshire and led what you would call a typical dog's life. His owners, a Mr and Mrs Greensmith, kept horses on their small holding, and there was a lovely orchard where Toby liked to go and play with the rabbits during the long summer evenings. He often amused himself like that as his owners were very busy people. He didn't mind for the more he chased about outside the better he slept at night in his cosy wicker basket.

Although Mr and Mrs Greensmith were sometimes absent, there was a live in housekeeper, Mabel Tucker, accompanied by her husband, Fred Tucker, who managed the estate and garden. Toby was therefore always fed and dried when it rained. Toby had never really bonded with the Tucker's. They had their own dog known as Meg they doted over. Meg was a working terrier. Her job was to catch rats. Meg was often busy and Toby loved her, in fact he'd had a crush on her from his puppyhood but she was older than him and too busy to return his affections. Life went on.

One day Toby was snoozing in his basket to be awakened suddenly at the sound of a heated discussion between Mr and Mrs Tucker. Apparently there was talk of the possibility that the Greensmith's may have to 'let them go', although Toby didn't quite know where or that it actually meant the Tucker's losing their comfortable positions. Mr Greensmith had roared up the driveway in his classic gold Porsche, marched through the front door bellowing to his wife about figures and bankruptcy. Mrs Greensmith had cried. She'd dealt with the accounts through a trusted member of the family and had been assured that the business was lucrative. Toby didn't understand this strange talk and 'walkies' was never mentioned so he went back to sleep when all was finally quite.

The next couple of weeks were tense. Toby hated tension. Even Meg was curt towards him. The breaking point for Toby was to discover that Meg was seeing a neighbour's terrier and Mr Tucker said he thought they made a perfect match and hoped for puppies one day. This was too much to take and as he watched his owners putting suitcases in the Porsche ready to go away yet again, he knew there would be no comforting or pet talk so he ran away into the lonely autumnal countryside where the trees rustled their leaves warning Toby of the

The Badger cubs hide toby

winter to come. He didn't care and ran on. A robin flew down and sang to him that he'd forgotten his collar and where was he going anyway? Toby didn't answer, he merely looked at the robin with his big dewy brown eyes and the robin knew that Toby was going for good.

It had been early morning when Toby had set off. He'd drunk from the little stream in the woods but had no appetite. Eventually, all the familiar scents of home were left behind and Toby didn't know where he was. His paws were sore so he curled up in a woody glen to sleep in a warm patch of evening sunlight. His dreams were not peaceful but anxious. When he awoke he felt as though he'd had little rest but was forced to move on because now it was raining. He needed to find shelter.

Eventually he came upon a farm yard. Here there was a lovely hay barn with a large open window. Toby soon discovered that there were boxes piled beside a large barrel and these made for a good ladder as the barn door was padlocked for the night. The drop down from the window was further than he'd expected. He landed heavily into the hay bales which cushioned his fall. Here he curled up and slept. Come early morning, Toby still slept heavily. He didn't hear the farmer open up the barn or hear him whisper to his wife,
   "Well what have we here?"
   Toby only awoke at the feel of warm hands scooping him up as he was still half asleep. He was placed gently on a rug in the kitchen with a dish of chicken laid down beside him. Famished he ate the lot. At the sound of a large grandfather clock striking poor Toby was so afraid he bolted through the door and ran on into the wild woods. There had been no big clock at the Greensmith's house as the sound of ticking disrupted Mr Greensmith from his work. The sound of clocks Toby had therefore never known and to him the deep chimes were such that the end of the world might have finally come. He ran and ran until the farmhouse was lost from view. It was a little while before his heart ceased to pound. He was alone again. At least he was safe.

Over the next few days, Toby tried to copy the vixen's talent for hunting, though of course he was much smaller. He tasted field mushrooms, blackberries and generally managed somehow or other to survive. Then one night, there was much scuffling about. Curious, Toby followed the sounds to see who or what was making them. To his surprise he saw many badgers standing around what looked like a mound of leaves. As he ventured closer, one by one the badgers turned to go back up into their sett. Somehow or other, Toby got caught up in the procession and found himself being edged along up into the badger sett that had been used for many decades by generations of badgers.
   "Oh excuse me?" Toby said trying to get away but a large sobbing sow badger kept nosing him up the rump saying,
   "Come along dear, you're holding up the procession." Her eyes were too full of tears to notice Toby was not one of them. The other badgers also seemed absorbed in their melancholy task.
   "Sssh! No speaking. It's disrespectful," mumbled another badger.
   So that night, just before day break, Toby was shoved along and put to bed with maturing badger cubs who giggled at the sight of him for he lacked the white face stripes and wasn't really like them at all. But as you will know, giggling is quite contagious and soon Toby was giggling with them at the sheer absurdity of it all. He'd finally made some friends.

The three badger cubs explained that all badgers slept during the daytime and foraged for food by night. If Toby was going to stay with them, he'd have to get used to it. Toby thought it was quite exciting and when Old Mother Sow Badger came in to check on the cubs, Toby was hidden from her view until the cubs could decide what to do and whether or not to tell her of his presence. What would she say they wondered?

Toby & Molly talk to a Badger cub

The sett had just lost the eldest member of their community. Great Grandpa Badger had died peacefully at the grand old age of fourteen and everyone was sad at his passing over. He had been quite a character with many a good story to tell on a cold and blustery day when the cubs could not sleep. They missed him so but now Toby was filling an empty space that their Great Grandpa had left. There would be 'a quiet time' and the cubs would be expected to behave. Born last March, they were not yet a year old and still liked to chase about and jump on each other close by the sett. Sometimes the adults would join in as well and then it became real fun. Although the cubs were old enough to move on, they had decided to remain with the main sett, as was their right, since there was room and over-crowding was not an issue.

The next day a storm broke out and everyone was unsettled. One of the elder badgers came in to see the cubs. This badger was eight years old and was known for his vast experience and story telling. There wasn't much this badger hadn't seen over the years and so he told the cubs, who were as usual hiding Toby beneath their furry bodies, a story to settle them down.

"One cold and blustery winter's day……." he began and continued, "……….found all the badgers sound asleep. This was years ago but I remember it as if it happened yesterday. In the distance a hunting horn sounded and there were hounds baying. Their blood curdling cries seemed to come from all directions as the wind carried the noise hither and thither. We all kept still in the sett, not daring to move although it was safe to say that the Hunt had never bothered us badgers. That's was it was see, the Hunt, people on horse back following the hounds who were in turn chasing deer or a fox. It doesn't happen nowadays but it used to not so long ago."

"Anyway the sound of the Hunt drew closer and closer and what do you think happened next?" asked the Elder Boar Badger.

Well the cubs didn't know. They shook their heads eager for the outcome.

"There was a lot of scuttling about so I wandered up to the main entrance to see what was happening and what do you think? A fox had hidden himself in our sett!" The Elder Boar Badger was laughing now saying how clever the fox had been by out-smarting the Hunt.

"Anyway, I got chatting to the fox, who begged his pardon, and he told me another trick he used when he'd been chased on the other side of the valley. He said he'd rolled in cows mess to mask his scent to then cross the river and 9 times out of 10 the hounds wouldn't pick up on his scent so he'd get away. Now then, that's what you cubs have got to be now you're nearly full grown, smart like a fox and eat like a badger and you'll be the smartest strongest badgers in the land. You've got to know how to survive. Now tomorrow I'll tell you a proper story. Sleep well." said the Elder Boar Badger who promptly trundled back to his own quarters.

"Cor, I'd like to meet a fox!" said Toby in admiration and falling to sleep beside his furry companions. What a happy little group they were.

Toby did find that the badgers didn't venture out as much as he'd like during the winter months. Although badgers didn't hibernate, they fed very well and lived on their fat reserves much of the time. Therefore Toby, who wasn't built like a badger began venturing off for his own foraging excursions, often by day when the badgers slept. Since it was dry and sunny, the cubs had told Toby to go off for a day because the Elder Badgers would be making them all dry their beds out in the sun. It had been so wet that the sett was musty and their bedding had become damp. All the badgers would be taking turns at pushing their bedding out into the open air to dry and the cubs would find it difficult to hide Toby. Toby didn't mind and needed a good walk anyway so off he went.

Following the stream was jolly. Toby liked the way the water chatted over pebbles and stones that were rounded by the constant passing of water. He played with fallen leaves and joyed in the sunshine that warmed his back even though the air was crisp. In the distance he saw a cottage. The chimney was smoking so someone must be at home he thought. It brought back memories of his previous owners and he realised that in all the excitement this was the first time he'd really missed them.

Staring into the stream at his own reflection made him jump. He'd spent so much time with the badgers that he actually felt like one now. To see his true face brought home the fact that he was not and never would be a badger even though they were his friends for life. Toby was so caught up in his own imagination that he hadn't heard the approach of another Dachshund.
    "Hello. My name is Molly." Said the other dog and Toby was so surprised he almost fell into the stream.

Molly sniffed Toby curiously and he sniffed her. Then they played chase round and round and before Toby knew where he was she had led him back to her garden where her surprised mistress was collecting logs for the fire. Molly's mistress noticed Toby wasn't wearing a collar. She also thought he looked as though he'd been roughing it and with a heart felt sigh she told Molly to bring her friend inside, after all it was lunch time. The lady made a phone call to the local vet to see if anyone had lost their Dachshund. The vet said they'd look into it. So Molly and Toby settled beside the fire. Molly wanted to know all about him so they had a lot to woof about. Time seemed to fly by and both dogs felt as if they'd known each other forever. Toby had found his true love and however he could've once thought of Meg in this way almost seemed laughable now, but then Toby had never been if love in the proper sense before.

It seemed that Molly's mistress worked at home. There was always paperwork about and Toby wondered what she did. Molly said she didn't really know and that people came and went quite a bit, business people mainly and all to do with writing on bits of paper.

Later on that night the dogs were let out for a run before bedtime. Toby wanted to tell the badgers what had happened but Molly said there wouldn't be enough time and the best time to go would be early in the morning but Toby wasn't sure he'd be able to rouse the badger cubs attention then. He'd have to try. It was a lot nicer being well fed and snuggled up to Molly in her basket than it was snoozing out in the wilds and fighting for survival Toby decided. Toby slept like he'd never slept before. He dreamed he was back in the badger sett listening to the promised story the Elder Boar Badger would be telling the cubs now. He dreamed of their faces and then of his mistress and when he finally awoke he wasn't sure where he was until a long wet tongue licked his face. Safe, that's where he was.

Molly's mistress was dressed in a suit this morning. She fed the dogs and asked them to play in the garden today because she had a client coming.

"We'll be alright Toby. I've got a lovely kennel full of hay we can use if it rains but I don't think it will rain today." Molly mused.

A gold Porsche pulled up beside the cottage and a lady knocked on the door.

"That's our cue Toby. We can go and tell your friends you're safe and still be back before we're missed." Molly said and off they went.

The Dachshunds ran along beside the stream and up into the woods. It was quite a long way for short little legs but it was surprising how quickly they covered the distance. Toby nodded towards the sett. Old Mother Sow Badger was pushing her bedding back into the sett and there was no chance Toby could get in through the tunnels to get a message to the cubs. The dog's waited hopefully but he didn't want to get the cubs into trouble for letting him sleep with them all this time. Molly and Toby were just about to go home when a sleepy eyed cub was pushing his bedding out into the sun to dry. He was being told off by Old Mother Sow badger for not doing it properly yesterday. When she went back inside with a huff, Toby approached the cub. He was so pleased to see Toby and glad to know he was well. The cub took one look at pretty Molly and jeered at Toby in light-hearted fashion.

"Arrrh, you've got a girlie whirlie friend" which made Toby blush and they all laughed. The cub understood and was pleased for him. Best of all the badgers would have two friends instead of one if ever the dogs wanted to come and play so all was well. The Elder Boar Badger seemed to have filled the shoes of Great Grandpa Badger, so missing him wasn't as bad as it used to be. Toby felt lighter now. He didn't want to let his friends down and he hadn't.

On returning home to Molly's garden the dog's played a noisy game of tug-o-war with one of Molly's toys. Little did they know that inside Mrs Greensmith was going through her accounts with Molly's owner who was in fact a Chartered Accountant.

"I'm sorry Mrs Greensmith, but your books have been totally mismanaged. I think we can save the business from bankruptcy though. You'll have to *deal* with your old accountant. I can't believe a member of you own family would do this. How awful! You have a right to prosecute but perhaps you'd better talk to your husband first." Molly's owner was telling Mrs Greensmith.

"I really can't thank you enough. I certainly owe Toby wherever he is. If the vet hadn't phoned to say a male Dachshund had been found, I would never have phoned you. I'd never have known we had a Chartered Accountant living close by and the business would have been lost. Oh it would be super if you have actually found my little dog. I do hope he hasn't run off again!" Mrs Greensmith sighed.

Molly's owner said not to worry because it sounded as if the dogs were back in the garden again.

"Molly never goes far," she said rising from her chair in order to call the dogs inside.

And what a fabulous reunion it was. Toby was invited to come and stay with Molly whenever the Greensmiths went away on business and now all would be well. The two lady dog owners would be seeing a lot of each other over the next few weeks and both agreed to let the dogs meet and play while they were busy dealing with business matters. Everything was going to be just fine!

THE END

Off to the Crystal Palace. From 'The Magnificent Adventures of Anne'.